**"Sophie isn't Riley. She didn't disappear without a trace. She left a trail."**

"You mean the text messages?"

"Among other things. We won't rest until we follow every bread crumb." Tom glanced over his shoulder at the house. "Your brother worries me, though. If he goes after the Moody boy, I'll have no choice but to lock him up."

"He was just letting off steam."

Tom's gaze was still on Rae. She didn't want to look up into those rain-colored eyes, but she couldn't help herself. He moved in, not so close as to be threatening, but enough so that the space between them grew intimate. She could almost imagine his hand on her arm, his knuckles scraping softly against her cheek. *Everything will be all right, Rae.*

Instead, he said, "I'm not your enemy. You need to trust me."

She let out a slow breath, releasing the anger she'd been harboring for hours. Not at Tom this time, but at her brother. At her niece's abductors. At her feeling of helplessness. "I'm trying to. I want to trust you. It's just..."

"My sister came home and yours didn't."

# WITHOUT A TRACE

## AMANDA STEVENS

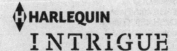

**HARLEQUIN**

INTRIGUE

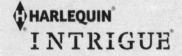

ISBN-13: 978-1-335-13584-1

Without a Trace

This edition published by arrangement with Harlequin Books S.A.

For questions and comments about the quality of this book, please contact us at CustomerService@Harlequin.com.

Harlequin Enterprises ULC
22 Adelaide St. West, 40th Floor
Toronto, Ontario M5H 4E3, Canada
www.Harlequin.com

Printed in U.S.A.

Recycling programs for this product may not exist in your area.

**Amanda Stevens** is an award-winning author of over fifty novels, including the modern gothic series The Graveyard Queen. Her books have been described as eerie and atmospheric, and "a new take on the classic ghost story." Born and raised in the rural South, she now resides in Houston, Texas, where she enjoys binge-watching, bike riding and the occasional margarita.

### Books by Amanda Stevens

#### Harlequin Intrigue

*An Echo Lake Novel*

Without a Trace

*Twilight's Children*

Criminal Behavior
Incriminating Evidence
Killer Investigation

Pine Lake
Whispering Springs

Bishop's Rock (ebook novella)

#### MIRA Books

*The Graveyard Queen*

The Restorer
The Kingdom
The Prophet
The Visitor
The Sinner
The Awakening

Visit the Author Profile page at Harlequin.com.

# CAST OF CHARACTERS

*Rae Cavanaugh*—When her teenage niece, Sophie, goes missing, Rae is forced to turn to the man she blames for her sister's disappearance fifteen years ago. She's willing to put the past behind them, but an unexpected phone call forces her to keep a secret that threatens their tenuous bond.

*Tom Brannon*—Fifteen years ago, three girls went missing after entering an abandoned psychiatric hospital. Tom's sister came back; Rae's didn't. He has borne the brunt of her family's misplaced anger and resentment for years. Now he must convince Rae to put all that aside for the sake of her missing niece.

*Preacher*—Has the monster presumed to have taken Riley Cavanaugh all those years ago come back for her niece?

*Jackson Cavanaugh*—The missing girl's father has a lot to answer for, including his daughter's depleted trust fund.

*Lauren Cavanaugh*—Sophie's glamorous stepmother has amassed a huge gambling debt.

*Dylan Moody*—Did Sophie's jilted boyfriend cook up the game that lured her to the Ruins the night she vanished?

*Hannah Tucker*—The betrayed best friend is a little too quick to point fingers.

# Chapter One

On the night of the disappearances, a blood moon had hovered over the piney woods in East Texas. The old-timers called it an omen. Tom Brannon had considered it just plain bad luck. He'd forgotten his flashlight when he rushed out of the house and the lunar eclipse provided weak illumination as he'd traipsed along the banks of the lake, hoping against hope that by the time he got back home, he'd find the girls safe and sound in his sister's bedroom.

Fifteen years had passed since that fateful night, but Tom still got a chill when the moon turned ruddy and a pine-scented breeze blew in from the lake. He stood outside the sheriff's station gazing up at the sky, telling himself to get back to work and forget about that moon. He had more important things to worry about at the moment, like budget cuts and rising crime rates, not to mention the mountain of complaints that seemed to grow exponentially higher with each passing day. On and on it went. The job of a rural county sheriff never ended.

He thought about his sister, Ellie, out there alone on Echo Lake. Miles from town. Miles from anyone. He'd asked her once if she ever got lonely, but she'd scoffed at the notion, insisting that the isolation kept her sane. Besides, it was only a twenty-minute drive into town, where she could find all the company she wanted. She seemed content these days, but Tom had to wonder if the nightmares ever came back. If she hid under the bed or at the back of her closet until the monsters went away. He didn't ask. He and his sister were close, but there were things they didn't talk about. Of the three girls who had entered the old hospital ruins on the night of the blood moon, Ellie was the only one who had come out whole. Survivor's guilt could be a powerful thing. Tom understood only too well.

Maybe it was the moon or maybe he was being overly protective, but he felt the need to check in with her tonight, hear her voice to calm his disquiet. He should have called earlier. She'd already be on the air by this time. She produced and hosted a syndicated radio program called *Midnight on Echo Lake*, which she broadcast from a small studio behind her house. She wouldn't answer her cell right now, but he could call in to the program. Talk about space aliens or the Bigfoot creature that some of the locals claimed to have seen in the woods near the lake. She'd get a kick out of that, though she'd later scold him for mocking her callers.

*Things happen that can't be explained*, she would tell him. People need someone they can talk to about their experiences without fear of ridicule.

*Yeah, and some people are just plain nuts*, Tom would retort.

Maybe he was one of them. He couldn't seem to shake the uneasiness that had gripped him all evening. He didn't believe in premonitions, but he knew enough to pay attention to his instincts. Something was brewing. He could feel it in the wind. He hoped it was nothing more than a summer storm.

"Evening, Sheriff."

He turned to find his newest recruit striding across the parking lot toward him. He checked his watch out of habit. The department ran on a six, two and ten schedule. Tom had been there since six that morning. He'd worked straight through two watches.

"You're early," he noted. "That's a good habit to get into."

"Yes, sir," the young officer replied with a solemn nod. A recent graduate of the East Texas Police Academy, Billy Navarro was a young, eager rookie who reminded Tom a bit of himself ten years ago. His father had been winding down his nearly thirty-year career as the Nance County sheriff when Tom had come on board. He'd served under his dad for only a year before a heart attack had claimed Porter Brannon in his sleep. Tom had then served under his father's replacement for another nine years, going from patrolman to criminal investigator to the deputy sheriff in less than a decade before running for office two years ago.

The campaign had gotten nasty and personal, fueled by a hostile opponent and an onslaught of negative commentary from the editorial pages of the *Echo Lake Star*. Everything from Tom's age to his integrity had been called into question, and there had been times when he wondered why he had ever thought it a good idea to try to follow in his father's footsteps. In the end, he'd won in a near landslide, no doubt a bitter pill to swallow for the Cavanaugh clan, who had spearheaded the campaign against him. He suspected the animosity between the two families would only worsen as the next election approached.

"Beware the blood moon," Billy muttered beside him.

Tom slanted him a frowning glance. "What did you say?"

"That's what my grandmother told me before

I left the house tonight." He shifted uneasily. "What kind of goodbye is that for a guy going out on patrol?"

"It's just an old wives' tale. Keep your eyes open and your mind on the job. You'll be fine."

Tom would never point out to a rookie that patrolling the town of Belle Pointe and the outlying country roads was hardly the same as taking on the mean streets of a crime-ridden city. He wanted Billy aware and on guard. Nance County was rural, but their home turf had more than its fair share of drug-related crime. Meth dealers had taken to scoping out abandoned houses in the country where they could cook their product in mass quantities. Then they used the nearby interstate to transport the drugs to points north and south. Big business. Big money. Synthetic weed was becoming a problem, too, along with fentanyl and the old standbys of crack cocaine and heroin.

Beside him, Billy searched the sky. "I know it's just a superstition, but there's something in the air tonight. Can you feel it?"

Yes, he felt it, but Tom didn't want to spook the rookie any more than he already seemed to be. He shrugged off his foreboding as he turned to go back inside. "Static electricity," he said. "Storm front moving in."

"There's not a cloud in the sky," Billy said.

"Not yet," Tom allowed. "Who's riding with you tonight?"

"Naomi Clutter."

"Tough as nails. Nobody better in three counties. You run into trouble, she'll have your back. You just make sure you have hers."

"Yes, sir."

Tom went back inside and crossed the nearly empty squad room to his glassed-in office at the front of the building. Long windows looked out on the street. He kept the blinds open so that he could see all around him, both within and without. The space hadn't changed much since his dad's time. The desk was the same. The vinyl chairs that faced him had been there for decades. Even the pictures and citations on the walls brought back memories. Tom had been meaning to change things up, bring in a few personal touches, but he never seemed to have the time. Never enough time for anything these days. He couldn't remember when he'd last asked a woman to dinner or a movie. He lived in town with neighbors all around him and yet in recent months he'd become as isolated as his sister.

He rubbed the bridge of his nose and then his temples. A headache nagged and exhaustion had set in, but paperwork kept him chained to his desk. Settling in with a fresh cup of coffee, he opened the latest budget report. The hours passed by quietly. He didn't take a break until right around midnight when he got up to stretch his legs.

When the call came in about the missing girl, he was standing at the window staring up at the moon.

RAE CAVANAUGH FINISHED loading the dishwasher and then wiped down the counters and set the timer on the coffee maker. She hated doing kitchen chores so late, but she'd fallen asleep after dinner in front of the TV. The house was so quiet and peaceful tonight. A welcome respite. She'd been burning the candle at both ends for as long as she could remember. A little downtime was just what she'd needed.

Her niece, Sophie, had roused her when she came in a few minutes ago. The girl had muttered a good-night and then gone straight upstairs to her room. Normally, music would be blasting through her closed door, but Sophie had seemed a bit subdued. Maybe she was coming down with something. Or maybe she'd had a fight with her boyfriend. Hard to tell with a sullen teenager.

Rae wondered if she should go up and try to talk to her, but she discarded the notion almost immediately. One, she was too tired to cope with the girl's moods, and two, she wanted to give Sophie her space. Wasn't that the whole point of this prolonged visit? To allow Sophie and her parents a much-needed breather?

Rae knew things must have gotten bad at her brother's house if he'd come to her for help. At his wit's end, he'd said. She'd never known Jackson to admit defeat, let alone to her. They'd been in bitter competition with one another since childhood. It didn't help that she'd always been their dad's favorite, but West Cavanaugh's partiality toward his daughter hadn't kept him from handing over the reins of Cavanaugh Industries to his only son. Rae was the chief financial officer—a glorified bookkeeper, she sometimes thought. Between the job and looking after their father, she had her hands full. And now Sophie. Poor kid. None of this was her fault. Rae blamed her brother and sister-in-law for letting things get so out of control. They'd lavished everything but attention on the girl without bothering to set boundaries. Now they were at loggerheads, with Sophie pushing for more independence and Jackson realizing a little too late that his princess might be headed for trouble.

Rae poured herself a glass of wine and took it out to the backyard, but she left the drink untouched as she gazed up at the moon. *What a strange night.* She felt unaccountably uneasy, and it wasn't just the argument she'd had earlier with Jackson or the troubling discrepancies she'd found in the financials. Or even the lawsuit that had been brought against Cavanaugh Industries by a neighboring rancher. That would all be sorted out soon enough.

Nothing Rae could do about any of it tonight. Her father would handle the lawsuit. He had a way of coming out of these things smelling like a rose. He and Jackson had spent untold hours sequestered with their corporate attorneys, discussing possible witnesses and devising strategy. Rae, of course, had been kept out of the loop, which suited her fine. Plausible deniability in case things went south.

She glanced up at her niece's window. The lights were out but she could see a muted glow from the laptop screen. Time for her to turn in as well, Rae decided. She carried the glass back into the kitchen and poured the wine down the drain before taking one last look at the eclipse through the window. Then, turning off the lights, she went upstairs, pausing on the landing to listen for any sign of life from Sophie's room. She could hear music playing, softly this time, and the murmur of Sophie's voice as she talked to someone on her cell. Rae didn't bother knocking or calling out. *Let the girl have her privacy.*

In her own room, Rae collapsed on top of the bed fully dressed and threw an arm over her eyes. She'd get up in a minute, wash her face and brush her teeth, but right now she just wanted to drift. Forget about Sophie down the hallway and her brother off on a deep-sea fishing trip with his buddies. His wife, Lauren, had gone down to New Orleans to visit friends. Now that they didn't have to worry about their daughter, they were footloose and fancy-free. Rae tried not to begrudge them a carefree weekend. She tried not to condemn their selfishness and poor parenting skills. *God knows after Mother died, I certainly failed Riley.*

Beautiful, smart, tenderhearted Riley. Rae's younger sister by two years. The girl who had entered the old hospital ruins on that fateful night fifteen years ago and had never been seen or heard from again.

Riley and her best friend, Jenna Malloy, had spent the night at Ellie Brannon's house. The parents had been called away on an emergency and Tom had been left in charge. He'd been sixteen when it happened. Same age as Rae. Old enough to know that you didn't go out partying when you were supposed to be minding the store. Never mind that the girls had been fourteen, also old enough to know better. Tom had been the one left in charge. He should have kept them safe.

Over the years, Rae had come to accept that her feelings toward Tom Brannon were at best irrational and at worst malicious, but old grudges never really died. They just crawled off into some back corner of the mind and waited.

She rolled over in bed, hugging her pillow as she stared out the window. She could see the moon through the pine trees. A blood moon, just as it had been on that night fifteen years ago. Rae wouldn't think about that now. She wouldn't think about her sister, Riley, and how much she still missed her. How much she would always miss her.

But it was Riley's smiling face she saw when she closed her eyes. It was Riley's anguished cry for help that echoed in her dreams when she finally fell asleep.

SOPHIE WAS TEMPTED to use the flashlight app on her phone, but there were houses on the lake and she didn't want to attract attention. The moon was up, dulled by a lunar eclipse, according to her science teacher. Sophie didn't much care about the reason. She just wished she could see where she was going as she made her way along the bank toward the Ruins, a hollowed-out shell of a building that had once housed a psychiatric hospital. Or so rumor had it. That was long before Sophie's time.

The place had always been spooky, but more so after those girls had gone missing. Sophie hadn't been born yet when her aunt had vanished from the Ruins. Ellie Brannon had come back. Jenna Malloy had eventually come back—at least physically—but Riley Cavanaugh had disappeared without a trace that night. And now here Sophie was, fifteen years later, headed for the same destination.

She wasn't frightened. Not really. The lake looked eerie in the muted moonlight, with cypress stumps rising from the shallow water and the banks curtained with Spanish moss. But as far as Sophie was concerned, there were scarier things back in town. Still, she couldn't help glancing over her shoulder now and then.

Her aunt Rae had been sound asleep when she'd slipped down the stairs and out of the house. Sophie couldn't get her license for another few months, so she'd ridden her bike out to the lake bridge and abandoned it beneath the supports. She had to go the rest of the way on foot. She was almost there now. She could see the smokestack from the old boiler room rising above the treetops. That gave her pause. So creepy. She was starting to get a little nervous now. She always did when her turn came, but she would never admit her unease to the others.

A twig snapped behind her and she whirled, peering all along the edge of the lake and into the woods. Nothing stirred except for the sway of the moss in the breeze and the gentle lap of water against the bank. A mosquito buzzed her face and she waved a hand to shoo it away. She should have brought insect repellent, but too late now.

She remained motionless for another long moment before turning back to the path. Up the steep bank she climbed, clutching vines and roots to help propel her to the top. When she reached the summit, she stood with the lake at her back and the Ruins silhouetted before her. Three stories of crumbling brick and mortar and broken-out windows.

Drawing a resolved breath, she picked her way through the weeds and brambles and entered through one of the arched doorways. Taking out her phone, she used the flashlight to illuminate the interior. She'd been here many times before, always in daylight until lately. She knew about the gurneys and wheelchairs that had been abandoned at the back of the building. She knew about the open elevator shaft upstairs and the caged area on the third floor. She angled the light beam over the biblical graffiti on the walls and the mural with the demonic face that had been painted on the ceiling.

*Preacher.* That was the name given to the former psychiatric patient who had continued to sermonize from his makeshift pulpit long after the hospital had closed down and the patients without families or financial means had been left to their own devices. Some had assimilated into nearby towns, or so the story went, but Sophie thought that might be another urban legend.

Whatever. She was here now. *Let the game begin.*

She crept from room to room, playing the light over the walls as she searched for a symbol that would guide her to the next level. The roof was missing in places and she had an image of the whole structure toppling down upon her, burying her in an avalanche of dark secrets and old misery. Would her aunt Rae blame herself? Would her parents? Would they even care?

The softest of steps sounded behind her. Phantom footfalls that sent a shiver down her spine. She turned slowly, the light beam capturing a silhouette for one split second before the shadow darted away.

Rae tried to swallow away her fear as she drew a quick breath. "Preacher," she said in a small voice. "Is that you?"

RAE AWAKENED WITH a start. She wasn't sure what had roused her this time. In her dream, someone had been pounding on the front door. She lay still for a moment, listening to the dark house, but the only noise she heard was the scratch of a tree limb against her window.

She crawled out of bed and headed for the bath-

room, then paused in midstride as her gaze went
to the bedroom door. She was certain she'd closed
it earlier, but now it hung open, as if someone had
stood in the hallway peering in at her.

Which was crazy. If Sophie had needed something, she would have barged right on in, turned
on the light and called Rae's name until she woke
up. The girl could be as subtle as a sledgeham-
mer at times. Still, Rae thought about her niece's
wan expression when she'd come home earlier.
Something had obviously been bothering her, and
now Rae regretted that she hadn't been a little
more curious.

She went down the hallway and listened at Sophie's door. She could hear music inside. Maybe
the girl was still up, still in need of a sympathetic
ear. Rae knocked softly. When she didn't get a response, she knocked a little harder and then tried
the door. She expected to find it locked from the
inside, but to her surprise, the door swung in-
ward, revealing the usual mayhem and clutter.
Music played from the laptop on Sophie's bed.
The window was open, allowing the night breeze
to blow in. The lights were off except for a night-
light that burned from the adjoining bathroom.
Rae crossed the room and peeked inside, wincing
at the mess. Damp towels had been tossed into a
corner and the vanity was littered with cosmet-
ics. But no Sophie.

Apprehension tickled at the back of Rae's neck, but she told herself there was no cause for alarm. Sophie had probably gone down to the kitchen for a snack. Rae checked the hallway bathroom before heading downstairs, turning on lights as she went. Sophie wasn't in the living room, den or kitchen. Not in the downstairs bathroom or out on the screened back porch. She wasn't on the front porch, either, or in the detached garage. She wasn't anywhere.

*Don't panic.* She'd probably sneaked out of the house to meet her boyfriend.

Disregarding the late hour, Rae called the kid's house, rousing his dad, who gruffly assured her that Dylan was in his room and had been since he'd come home around ten. Rae insisted he go check to make sure, which he'd begrudgingly agreed to do. Then he'd put Dylan on the phone and the kid had sworn he hadn't seen Sophie since he'd dropped her off at home at 10:00 p.m.

Rae sat out on the front porch and called everyone else she could think of. None of Sophie's friends had seen her. No one knew anything. How could she have slipped out of the house without Rae knowing? She was usually such a light sleeper.

*Okay, just stay calm. It's not that late.* A few minutes after midnight. Well past curfew for a school night but Sophie wasn't one for following the rules. Rae tried the girl's cell phone for the umpteenth time and then sent her a barrage of text messages.

Where are you?

I'm starting to freak out a little. Call me as soon as you get this message. Just let me know you're okay.

Sophie, call me! Call me right this minute! I'm serious!

You're not in trouble, I promise. Just call me. I need to know you're okay.

Sophie, please call me.

I'm worried.

After a bit, Rae got up and went back inside. She climbed the stairs to Sophie's room and checked the laptop, then searched through the dresser drawers and closet looking for a clue as to where the girl might have gone. Then she got in her car and drove through town, up one street and down the other.

By the time she got back home, she could no longer keep panic at bay. It didn't matter that Sophie had been missing for only a couple of hours. It didn't matter that her niece had once pulled a similar stunt on her parents. Rae was responsible for the child now. She was the one in charge.

Plopping down on Sophie's bed, she sent off another volley of texts before reaching for the laptop once again. Then she called the last person on earth she had expected to talk to that night.

RAE CAVANAUGH WAS the last person Tom had expected to hear from that night...or ever. He automatically checked his watch when the call came in. He should have left for home an hour ago, but he supposed it was just as well that he hadn't. No matter the time, a call from a Cavanaugh would have been forwarded to his cell phone or landline. They were important folks, the Cavanaughs, and they weren't shy about letting you know it.

He figured the call had something to do with the kid he had in lockup, one of their young roughnecks who'd gotten himself into a little trouble earlier in the evening. Tom wasn't in the mood to be raked over the coals, but he could face Rae's wrath now or in the morning. Didn't much matter to him. He'd developed a thick skin when it came to the Cavanaughs.

"Sheriff Brannon." He answered the phone in his usual manner, fully expecting a surly comeback.

"This is Rae Cavanaugh."

She sounded out of breath. Distressed. Tom frowned. "What can I do for you, Rae?"

"Sophie's gone missing."

The unease that had niggled all evening deepened. "Sophie?"

"My niece. Jackson's daughter. She's been staying with me for a while. I went to check on her earlier and she's not in her room. I called everyone I could think of. All her friends, her boyfriend. No one has seen her. Tom…" He could imagine her clutching the phone as everything she'd done to find her niece came pouring out in her panic. When she finished, she took another moment to gather her poise. "You and I have had our differences in the past, but I didn't know who else to call. I don't know what else to do. I've looked everywhere. She's not answering her phone or my texts. I just keep thinking about that night—"

"Hold on," he said. "You say she came home at ten and went up to her room. It's just after midnight now. At most she's only been gone a couple of hours. Teenagers sneak out of the house all the time."

"I know that. I keep telling myself she's just gone off with a friend, but I checked with the girls I know she's close to. No one has seen her."

"Maybe she has a friend you don't know about."

"It's possible. She hasn't been living with me that long, Tom." Dread crept into her voice. "I found something on her laptop just now. She has dozens of pictures of the Ruins. I think she took them herself. They look recent. You don't think—"

"I was just leaving the office. I'll make a run out there before I head home."

"I'm coming, too. It'll be faster if I meet you there."

"Maybe you should stay home in case she comes back," he said.

"I'll leave a note and I'll take my cell phone. I can't sit in this house and do nothing. I'll go crazy with worry."

He sighed under his breath. "Okay, but if you get there first, wait for me by the bridge. Don't go any farther without me. Understand?"

"Tom…"

"What is it?"

She hesitated. "Aren't you going to say it?"

"Say what, Rae?"

"This is my fault. She's my responsibility."

"Let's just find her and bring her home."

Tom ended the call and then went out to the squad room to speak with the dispatcher. A patrol car would meet them at the bridge. They could all traipse through the woods together. Most likely, the girl was out partying somewhere, but Tom didn't take chances with missing kids.

As he went out to his own vehicle, he couldn't help glancing skyward once more. The moon had disappeared behind a storm cloud.

## Chapter Two

Rae's car was pulled to the side of the road by the time Tom got out to the lake. He half expected she'd already taken off for the Ruins alone, but he called out to her anyway. To his surprise, she answered back immediately.

"Down here!"

He used his flashlight to pick his way down the embankment, half running, half sliding in the loose dirt and pebbles. His light flicked across Rae. She stood at the edge of the lake peering up under the bridge. His heart skidded but he kept his voice calm as he greeted her.

"Glad you waited for me."

"I found her bike," she said over her shoulder. She used her flashlight beam to guide his attention. "See it up there under the braces?"

"You sure it's hers?"

"I'm certain. She brought it with her when she came to stay with me."

"How long has that been?"

"Nearly three weeks. There was trouble at home," she admitted reluctantly.

"What kind of trouble?"

"The usual stuff. Jackson doesn't approve of her friends or the way she dresses or the music she listens to, and you know how well criticism goes over with a teenager. Even under the best of circumstances, Sophie's a handful and my brother has never been the most tactful or patient person in the world. They all needed a break."

"So you came to the rescue." Tom hadn't meant anything by the comment, but he regretted how it might sound to her.

"I offered to help. That's what families do."

"The good ones." As he turned to scan their surroundings, his light caught her again. She seemed unaware of his quick scrutiny. The bike had her full attention. She looked uncharacteristically unkempt, her light brown hair tangled down her back, freckles exposed across her nose, clothing rumpled. Understandable under the circumstances. She'd undoubtedly left the house in a hurry, but what Tom couldn't help noticing was that her frayed demeanor did little to disguise her appeal. He'd always admired Rae Cavanaugh's good looks if not her disposition. As far back as high school, she'd been a real piece of work. Prickly, suspicious and obnoxiously competitive.

Riley had been the sweet one. It pained Tom even now to think about her.

He kept his voice neutral as he asked the necessary questions. "You two didn't have an argument, did you? Maybe she left the house to cool off. Or to teach you a lesson. Kids are like that."

"We didn't fight. We've been getting along reasonably well, considering."

"Considering?"

"Like you said, she's a kid. I don't have a lot of experience dealing with teenagers except for…" She trailed off.

*Except for Riley.*

Tom finished her sentence in his head. Their mother had died when the Cavanaugh kids were still young. West Cavanaugh had remarried a few years later and there'd been a string of nannies and housekeepers in between. But Rae was the one who had looked after Riley. She'd been fiercely protective of her sister, so much so that Riley had taken to spending all her free time at their house just so she could have a little breathing room.

Tom wondered if Rae ever thought about that in those late hours when she couldn't sleep. He wondered if she remained so hard on him because it was easier to attack than to reflect.

A car engine sounded on the road. Doors slammed and voices carried down to the lake.

He called out to the patrol officers and both Billy Navarro and Naomi Clutter responded. A moment later, their flashlight beams bobbed in the dark as they hustled down the embankment.

Tom made short work of the introductions and explanations. Then they left the bridge and the abandoned bike and headed toward the Ruins, dread dogging their every step. Tom told himself it was much too early to worry. Two hours, going on three was nothing in the life of a teenager, especially one who might be acting out because of a difficult home life. He didn't know Jackson and Lauren Cavanaugh well, but he'd had enough run-ins with the former to know that he could be a real jerk. The wife appeared to be the high-maintenance type, and Tom could well imagine how a spirited teenage stepdaughter might get in the way of spa treatments and country-club luncheons. Not a fair assessment, he readily admitted, but he wasn't inclined to be all that generous when it came to the Cavanaughs.

None of that mattered at the moment anyway. *Just find the girl and we'll sort the rest out later.*

The eclipse had entered its final stage. The moon drifted from behind a cloud, glimmering like quicksilver on the surface of the lake. Somehow the illumination made the woods all around them seem darker, thicker. No one said much. Billy and Naomi had taken the lead, Rae trailed behind them and Tom brought up the rear. He couldn't stop thinking about that night fifteen years ago when he'd raced along the water's edge alone. He couldn't help brooding about the outcome.

Rae slowed and fell into step beside him. "Your sister lives out here somewhere, doesn't she?"

"Her house is on the other side of the bridge." Tom glanced over his shoulder. "If you look close enough, you can see the lights on her antenna flickering through the pine boughs."

"I've listened to her show a few times. She has a soothing voice, but her callers are pretty strange," Rae said. "Where do those people come from anyway? Are they for real?"

"She gets the occasional prank call, but most of them are real and they call in from all over the place. They just need somebody to listen to their story. At least, that's what Ellie tells me."

"I don't see her in town much anymore. How is she?"

"She's fine. Busy. Likes her solitude."

Rae shivered as she glanced over the water and then turned her head and gazed up at what could be seen of the Ruins. "I would go crazy out here."

"The Cavanaugh ranch is pretty isolated," Tom pointed out.

"That's different. People are always around. My dad, the housekeeper and all the ranch hands coming and going. It's like a small town out there. One of the last big cattle ranches in the area," she said proudly.

And quintessentially East Texas, Tom thought as he conjured an image of an Angus herd grazing peacefully in lush green pastures dotted with pumper jacks. The peaceful scenery in his head was a far cry from the disturbing reality of their current surroundings. Echo Lake held too many bleak memories, too many deep, dark secrets.

As if reading his thoughts, Rae glanced out over the water with a shiver. "I've heard people say that when the air is still and the hour is late, you can hear the screams of the patients echoing across the water. I never put much stock in all those old legends, but being out here like this... One can imagine almost anything."

"Most likely what they hear are the peacocks from the old Thayer place," Tom said. "They've roamed the countryside ever since Mrs. Thayer passed. My sister walks over a few times a week to feed them."

Up ahead, Billy and Naomi had already begun the ascent to the top of the embankment. Tom knew better than to offer Rae assistance. She was too proud to accept his hand. Instead, she propelled herself up to the summit like a seasoned climber and stood waiting for him to scramble up behind her. Then they all took a moment to gaze at the Ruins.

Moonlight glinted off the windows, giving the place a strange sense of animation. Of being alive. Tom scoffed at himself. Maybe Rae's trepidation had rubbed off on him. Maybe he was letting his own imagination get the better of him because if he listened closely enough, he could hear the creak of a door somewhere inside. Or was that the squeal of a rusted gurney? With very little effort, he could conjure ghostly images behind the broken windowpanes and phantom whispers rippling down through the trees. He shook off those visions, reminding himself that a place couldn't be evil or haunted. The only real monsters were human.

"We'll check around back," Naomi said.

Tom nodded. "We'll take the front. Call out if you find anything."

"Roger that."

She and Billy headed off into the darkness and Tom turned to Rae. "Are you sure you don't want to wait for me outside?"

"No, I need to go in with you. If Sophie's inside and she sees you come in alone, she might get scared and think she's in trouble. I don't want to take the chance that she could run off again."

She had a point. "Okay, but we need to stick together. And watch your step. I don't trust the integrity of this place. One wrong move and the whole structure could come down on top of us."

"It's been standing for decades," Rae said. "Even been through a few tornadoes. I think we're safe enough, but your point is taken. I'll be careful."

They entered through one of the archways, pausing to rake their flashlight beams over the graffiti.

"I always wondered what this place was like on the inside. It's even creepier than I imagined," Rae said in a hushed voice. Her light lingered on the ceiling mural. "What's that?"

"Preacher." Tom swept his light over the demonic fresco. The eyes seemed to glow, but he knew that was only an illusion of paint and moonlight. "So you've never been inside before? That's surprising. Spending time at the Ruins has been a rite of passage in these parts ever since the place closed down."

"I was never much of a follower, and then after Riley disappeared…" She trailed away. "I've been outside plenty of times, but I could never make myself enter. After it happened, I'd drive out after school and walk around the area calling my sister's name even though I knew she was long gone. I tried to picture where she might be. Tried to put myself in her place, imagine her fear, her screams…"

Tom heard a tremor in her voice. He was having flashbacks of that night, too. He'd been so panicked by the time he entered the building, he hadn't stopped to assess the risk. On some level, he'd been aware of the structural danger and the possibility of rattlers or copperheads, but the human menace had eluded him until he heard the softest of footfalls behind him. By then it was too late. He was struck across the back of his head, so hard he fell to his knees. Another blow knocked him out cold.

He came to the next morning at the bottom of the rise, his hair and clothing stained with blood. He'd been rolled down the embankment and left for dead, no doubt bleeding so profusely that the assailant hadn't bothered to finish him off. Tom had found Ellie lying facedown at the water's edge. How she'd gotten away from her attacker or why she hadn't drowned was anyone's guess. Tom had administered CPR and then carried her all the way to the bridge, up the embankment and out to the road where he'd left his vehicle the night before.

Eighteen stitches and a week in the hospital later, he'd still blamed himself for not being able to save the others, even though he knew in his gut that Riley and Jenna had already been taken by the time he regained consciousness.

Beside him, Rae froze as she angled her beam along the cracked floor tiles. "Tom, look at this."

He came over to stand beside her. Then he squatted, focusing his light on the red droplets.

"Is that blood?" she asked fearfully.

He touched his finger to a drop. "It's fresh, but there isn't much of it. Let's not jump to conclusions." Too late for that. He heard the sharp intake of Rae's breath as she swung the flashlight wildly around the crumbling interior, tracking up the stairs and searching in all the dark corners.

"Sophie! Are you in here? Sophie, it's Rae. Answer me!" He heard another gasp. "I saw something!"

He rose. "Where?"

She positioned the light at the top of the stairs. "Someone was up there watching us. A man, I think."

"Stay here." Tom unholstered his weapon as he moved toward the stairs. Running the flashlight beam along the landing, he started up, testing each step with his weight before moving on to the next. When he got to the top, he angled the beam down the long corridor, taking note of open doorways and piles of debris, places from which he could be ambushed.

"Sophie!" he called out. "Are you up here? This is Sheriff Brannon. You're not in any trouble. Your aunt is with me. We just want to make sure you're okay." Gun in his right hand, flashlight in his left, he eased down the corridor, shining the beam inside the empty rooms. He heard footsteps on the stairs. "Rae, is that you?"

"I'm coming up," she said.

He didn't bother to argue. "Watch your step. The floor is rotting through up here."

He heard her behind him, but he didn't turn. Up ahead, in one of the gloomy recesses, he'd caught the glimmer of human eyes. "Whoever you are, put your hands behind your head and come out where I can see you." Rae was at the top of the stairs now. He said over his shoulder, "Stay where you are, Rae."

"Who's up here?" she asked on a breath.

"I don't know yet. Stay by the stairs."

In front of him, a shadow darted across the corridor. Startled, Tom called out, "Freeze!"

A face peered back at him for a split second before disappearing. Just vanished before Tom's very eyes.

He moved forward cautiously until one foot found nothing but air. He found himself teetering on the brink of the old elevator shaft. A rope swung wildly from a rafter as if someone had rappelled down into the chute. He leaned over the opening, allowing the flashlight beam to peel away the inky layers. Something was down there, crumpled on the floor.

"Tom?"

He threw out an arm to halt Rae's progress. "Careful. Long drop. Looks like it may go all the way down to the basement."

"What is it?"

"The old elevator shaft. Someone's rigged up a rope. I think whoever was up here used it to lower himself down."

Tom holstered his weapon and reached for the rope, rocking precariously for a moment before Rae grabbed his arm and pulled him back. "Are you crazy? You don't know how old that thing is. Who knows how much weight it'll hold."

She was right. A broken leg wouldn't help them find Sophie. "Let's see if we can figure out another way into the basement."

They backtracked along the corridor, down the stairs and through a maze of hallways to the back of the building. Outside, Tom glanced once again at the sky. The eclipse was nearly over. He wanted to take that as a good sign, but the blood drops inside, coupled with the crumpled form he'd seen in the elevator shaft, didn't bode well for a happy outcome. Beside him, Rae remained tense and silent.

He could see the deputies' flashlight beams bobbling in the dark. He called out to them. "Stay alert. We saw someone inside."

"Any sign of the girl?" Naomi called back.

"Not yet. We're looking for a way down into the basement. One of you stand guard out here, the other go around to the front. Make sure no one leaves this place without our knowing."

They split up, Billy taking the rear while Naomi went around to the front. Tom and Rae searched along the house until they located the outside basement entrance. A set of concrete steps led down to a metal door that hung open on one rusty hinge. He pulled back the door and then angled his flashlight beam into the cavernous space.

An odor of sour mud and dead fish emanated from the cellar, reminding Tom of a bog. He imagined there were plenty of rats and snakes in there, too. He didn't relish an exploration, but he wasn't about to delegate that job to a rookie.

He said over his shoulder, "You two wait out here. Keep your eyes peeled."

"I'm coming with you," Rae insisted. "Sophie is my niece. She's my responsibility. I need to help you find her." She touched his sleeve. "Please, Tom."

He stepped back. "Can you smell that? You still want to go in there?"

"I don't want to, no. I want to be back home asleep in my bed with Sophie safe and sound down the hallway. But I'm not leaving here until we've searched every square inch of this place."

"All right, then," he said. "Let's get it done."

RAE PUT THE back of her hand to her nose as she followed Tom into the basement. That smell! As if she hadn't been apprehensive enough. The stench of sour mud and rotting vegetation permeated her nostrils and clogged her throat. She swallowed past her gag reflex and braced herself. She had to do this. Now was not the time to go wimpy and squeamish. She had to find Sophie. Nothing else could be allowed to matter.

She cleared her throat, dropped her hand from her nose and took a few tentative breaths until she felt clearheaded and steady. The building was on high ground, but enough rainwater had seeped in over the decades to allow mold, mildew and all manner of creeping things to take up residence. Even now Rae could have sworn she heard dripping water, but they hadn't had rain in weeks. Maybe it was condensation. The air was damp, and the stone floor felt slippery beneath her sneakers.

She resisted the urge to cling to Tom's shirt as they made their way through small mountains of discarded equipment and debris. She didn't want to think about the original purpose of all those old contraptions, but already she had visions of restraints and drain tables dancing through her head. Once upon a time, the hospital had had its own morgue. She wondered if that was where they were now.

The elevator was just ahead. She tried to get a better view, but Tom's broad back kept blocking her, as if he wanted to shield her.

"What are you doing?"

He glanced over his shoulder. "What do you mean?"

"You keep moving in front of me. Why? What are you afraid I'll see?"

"I've got a weapon and you don't," he said. "We don't know who or what we'll find down here. It's best that you stay behind me."

"You saw something from above, didn't you?"

"I don't know what I saw," he admitted. "Will you just stay behind me?"

"You think Sophie's—"

"Alive," he said. "We've no reason to think otherwise."

"Except for the blood we found."

"A very small amount and could be animal blood, for all we know. Just stay focused. Let's finish this job."

They approached the elevator shaft and Rae moved around Tom despite his protests. Her heart thudded when her flashlight beam connected with something on the floor. Tom moved quickly to investigate.

"It's just a bunch of old clothing," he said.

Was that relief she heard in his voice? "Are you sure?"

He picked up a metal rod from the floor and prodded the pile. "See?"

No sooner had Rae let out her own relieved breath than a sound brought her up short. She couldn't identify the direction of the noise. The basement had an echo effect that disoriented her. Why had she insisted on coming down here with Tom? She could have remained outside with the officer and no one would have thought less of her. She hated close places. Hated the dampness even more. Hated the sensation that something or someone lurked in the shadows, just beyond the reach of her flashlight. Rae wasn't one for allowing her imagination to get the better of her, but this place held too many trapped memories.

Tom called to his deputy. "Billy?"

"Right here, sir." His voice came from the top of the outside steps.

"You see anything out there?"

"No, sir. Everything's quiet. What about down there?"

"We're about to find out," Tom said.

Rae moved her flashlight beam around the room. Near the entrance, something glinted.

"Tom?" Her voice was barely a whisper. "Someone's down here."

Icy fingers slid down her back as she gripped the flashlight. She used her other hand to steady her wrist as she vectored in on a silhouette.

Human. Tall, lanky with longish hair and a scraggly beard. She thought for a moment her fear had conjured the man, but then she caught the glimmer of his beady eyes before he dropped to the floor and scurried crab-like back into a yawning black hole beside the entrance.

"Did you see—"

Tom swore under his breath as he sprinted across the room, Rae at his heels. She wasn't about to be left behind.

A metal gate hung open, revealing the dark void into which the man had scuttled.

"What is that place?" she asked on a quavering breath.

Tom knelt to shine his light back into the opening. "Looks to be a crawl space or a tunnel of some sort. I can see some old pipes. Lots of cobwebs, too."

"You're not going in there," Rae said.

"Get Billy down here."

"Tom, you can't—"

"Make sure he knows where I'm going."

She didn't argue further, but spun on her heel and ran up the steps. She called to the deputy, told him about the tunnel, and by the time he'd followed her back into the basement, Tom had disappeared.

THE CRAWL SPACE went on and on. Tom walked hunched over, occasionally dropping to his hands and knees when the floor and ceiling tightened. He'd never been bothered by close places, but the tunnel unnerved him. It was damp and moldy and he could smell something fetid up ahead. Something that churned his stomach and stiffened his backbone.

Dead rodents, he told himself, but the dark passenger of dread climbed upon his shoulder and whispered bad things in his ear. He shook off the presentiment, reminding himself that Sophie had been missing only a few hours. For all they knew, she was out partying with a friend or lying low someplace to teach her parents a lesson. No reason to believe the worst. They still had plenty of time.

But the clock was ticking and the crawl space seemed endless. After a bit, Tom felt a slight ascension, as if he were heading back up to ground level.

Rae called out to him. His muffled name reverberated through the narrow passage, sending a shiver down his spine even as he took comfort in the sound of her voice. "Just stay put," he called back to her.

He didn't know if she'd heard him or not. Surely she wouldn't try to follow him through the crawl space. He couldn't worry about that right now, though. He had to follow this thing to the end, had to discover the source of that smell.

He plunged on, eventually arriving at another gated opening. Instead of getting closer to the source of the smell, the odor had faded. He could feel fresh air on his face. The crawl space had led him from the main building back to the old boiler room. Tall windows allowed in enough moonlight so that he could make out the metal grates that would have restricted the flames.

Perching at the edge of the opening, he shone his flashlight into the room before he dropped down to the floor and stood gazing around. The space was littered with discarded food cans, an old mattress and what looked to be a camping stove. Someone had been living there.

He caught a movement out of the corner of his eye and turned just as an emaciated man with a heavy beard leaped out of the crawl space and flung himself at Tom, knocking him off balance. He swore as he scrambled to his feet. Once he regained his equilibrium, he had no trouble fending off the scrawny attacker.

"That's enough," Tom said, holding the flailing assailant at bay. Then he pushed him away and the man dropped to the floor, cowering and whimpering.

"I didn't do nothing. You got no call to hurt me like that."

"You're the one who jumped me," Tom pointed out. "I was just defending myself."

The man cringed and hid his face.

"Look at me." Tom trained the flashlight beam on the badge he wore clipped to his belt. "My name's Tom Brannon. I'm the Nance County sheriff. What are you doing in here? Have you been living in this place?"

The man sat up and scratched a bony arm. "I stay here sometimes when I'm passing through. No law against that, is there?"

"Depends on what you've been up to." Tom flicked the beam around the room. "What's your name?"

"Marty."

"You got a last name?"

"Booker."

"Have you seen anyone else at the Ruins tonight, Marty?"

"Like who?"

"A girl." Tom had been moving the flashlight around the room, but now he froze the beam on the floor. He used one of the disposable gloves he kept in his pocket to pick up a cell phone in a pink silicone case, gingerly holding it by the edges. "Where did you get this?"

"Found it."

"Where?"

Marty gave a vague nod toward the door. "Over yonder. Somebody dropped it, I reckon. Finders, keepers."

The phone wasn't locked. Tom kept an eye on the man while he scrolled through the contact numbers. Before he had time to get through the list, Rae burst through the door with Billy Navarro behind her.

"We saw a light out here and then we heard voices." She halted when she saw the stranger shrinking in the shadows. "Who's he?"

"Says his name's Marty Booker." Tom held up the phone. "Do you recognize this?"

Her eyes went wide with shock. "It's Sophie's. Where did you find it?"

"It was lying on the floor in plain sight." He handed the phone to Navarro. The deputy produced a plastic evidence bag, dropped the phone inside and sealed it.

"Lying on the floor in *here*?" Horror crept into Rae's tone. "Where did it come from?"

He nodded toward the man in the shadows. "That's what I'm trying to determine. He says he found it in the main building."

Rae took a step toward the stranger. "You saw Sophie tonight?" When he didn't respond, she advanced closer. "You took her phone, so you must have seen her. Where is she? *Where is she!?*"

The outburst startled even Tom. He had no doubt Rae would have gone for the man's throat if he hadn't caught her arm and held her back. She tried to shrug out of his grasp. "Let go of me!"

He held her tighter. "Settle down."

"But he knows something!"

In all the commotion, Marty Booker shrieked and buried his head in his arms.

Rae was unmoved. "If you've hurt my niece in any way, I swear to God I'll—"

"Just cool it," Tom warned. "We're not going to get anything out of him if you keep threatening him like that."

She jerked away. "Why aren't you doing anything?"

"I'm trying to do my job if you'd let me."

"That would be a first!" she shot back.

*Okay, truce over,* Tom thought. He wouldn't hold it against her under the circumstances.

Marty Booker took a peek from between folded arms, his gaze darting from Tom to Rae. "I didn't do anything, I swear it. I would never hurt anyone."

"But you saw a girl out here tonight," Tom said.

He hemmed and hawed before he shrugged. "Maybe I saw her."

"Where?" Rae demanded.

He gave the same vague nod toward the entrance. "I see them over there sometimes, but they don't see me."

Tom held up a hand to silence Rae. "Who?"

"Those kids. *Him.*"

"Him?"

Booker's eyes lifted to the ceiling as if he were searching for the mural. *"Him."*

Tom said to Rae, "Do you have a picture of Sophie?"

She fumbled for her phone and then scrolled through the camera roll.

Tom took the phone and held up the screen so that Booker could see the shot of Sophie. "Did you see this girl tonight?"

He hesitated. "Maybe it was her. I don't see so well at night."

"Do you know where she is now?"

"He took her."

"Who?" Tom pressed.

"Preacher," he whispered. "Preacher took that girl."

# Chapter Three

By morning, word had gotten out about Sophie Cavanaugh's disappearance and a small crowd had gathered outside the station waiting for news. Tom's deputies had returned to the Ruins at first light and were now scouring the building and surrounding area for evidence. The blood sample collected hours earlier at the scene had been sent to the lab for analysis, and Tom's IT specialist, a young deputy named Noah Goodnight, was going through Sophie's cell phone and laptop.

A call to the sheriff in the next county verified Marty Booker's claim that he had family living nearby. The sheriff was well aware of the man. "It's a sad story," he told Tom. "Suffered a severe head trauma when he was just a kid. Hasn't been right since, but as far as I know, he's never been violent. Just wanders around the countryside until he gets ready to come home."

Tom was inclined to agree. He didn't think Marty Booker was responsible for Sophie's disappearance, but he suspected the man had seen more than he was willing to admit. Scared, maybe. Or unable to process what he'd witnessed. Either way, spending the night in a holding cell hadn't done him any harm. If nothing else, he'd gotten a shower, clean clothes and a hot meal.

As for his claim that Preacher had taken Sophie, Tom wasn't sure what to make of that. Silas Creed hadn't been seen or heard around Nance County since Riley Cavanaugh and Jenna Malloy had gone missing. It was a widely held belief that Creed had taken the girls and held them captive in an abandoned house. Law enforcement personnel and untold volunteers had scoured the countryside for days. When Jenna Malloy had been found wandering down a rural road weeks after she'd been taken, she'd been in a near catatonic state, too emotionally fragile and confused to identify her abductor, let alone lead the police to where the girls had last been held. Jenna had spent the next fifteen years of her life in and out of psychiatric facilities. Tom had lost track of her a long time ago, but he sometimes wondered if Ellie still kept in touch.

He seriously doubted that Silas Creed had returned to Nance County after all this time. He'd be almost sixty by now. Most likely the man was long dead. However, Tom couldn't afford to discount any possibility. He pulled every file he could find on the previous abductions, noting with a pang his father's handwritten notes in some of the margins.

He had everything spread out in his office ready to dig in when he decided to take a ride over to Rae Cavanaugh's place. Things had gotten a little heated the night before and Tom knew he hadn't been as tactful as he should have been. He understood only too well that feeling of utter helplessness, and a part of him wanted to hang back and give her some space. But they were well into the critical twenty-four-hour window and Tom needed her cooperation and he needed her trust. Sophie's life could depend on it.

She lived in one of the town's older neighborhoods. Quaint and private. Unlike the newer subdivisions out by the interstate, all the houses here were different—tidy ranches, stately colonials, a few scattered Victorians. Rae's house was a white prewar bungalow with black shutters and flagstone walkways. Oak trees shaded the front yard, the gnarled branches hidden by whiskers of Spanish moss. The air was thick with the scent of roses. Belle Pointe was situated on the Texas-Louisiana border, and Tom had always thought his hometown more Southern than Texan, though there was no shortage of Lone Star spirit and pride in the area. Life was a little slower here, a little quieter until you probed beneath the surface. Until you remembered that young girls had gone missing.

He didn't recognize the car in her driveway when he pulled up. Rae drove a brand-new mid-size SUV and he doubted the aging coupe belonged to Jackson or Lauren Cavanaugh. Not their style. He took note of the license plate number and glanced inside the car as he walked up the driveway.

Rae answered the bell immediately, pulling back the door in anticipation before her expression fell when she saw him. She glanced past him to the street. "Have you found her?" The question was blunt, her tone filled with a heart-tugging mixture of hope and dread. Little wonder, given her previous experience.

"No. That's not why I'm here," Tom said. "I wanted to touch base. But I guess your reaction means you haven't heard from her, either."

She shook her head, looking bleak.

"I thought we could go back over everything that happened last night," he said. "Memories have a way of returning once the dust settles."

She stepped back and motioned him inside. "I don't know what more I can tell you, but it's certainly worth a try." She wore jeans, sneakers and a plain gray T-shirt. Her hair was pulled back into a careless ponytail and she hadn't bothered with makeup. "I was thinking about heading back out to the Ruins," she said. "I can't sit here all day and do nothing."

"I've got deputies combing the area. But organizing a search party isn't a bad idea." It might be a little early for that, but the abandoned bicycle and those drops of blood worried Tom. Not to mention Sophie's cell phone. At the very least, recruiting volunteers would give the family something to do.

"We're already on that." A girl Sophie's age appeared from another room. She walked up to Rae. "Sorry. I wasn't trying to eavesdrop, but I couldn't help overhearing."

"It's okay," Rae said. "Sheriff Brannon, this is Hannah Tucker, one of Sophie's friends."

"Her *best* friend," Hannah clarified as she extended her hand.

"Hannah came by first thing this morning," Rae explained. "She's been helping me compile a list of Sophie's friends, acquaintances, favorite hangouts. That sort of thing."

"Good idea." Tom shook the girl's hand and then followed Rae back to the kitchen, where she'd turned the breakfast table into a workspace. A teenage boy with dark hair and a brooding expression sat at the island with his laptop. He glanced up when they walked in and then did a double take when he recognized Tom. He ducked his head and averted his gaze just a little too quickly by Tom's measure.

"This is Dylan Moody, Sophie's boyfriend."

"Glad you're here," Tom said. "I'd like to ask you and Hannah a few questions if you don't mind."

"Is that legal?" Hannah asked. "We're both minors. Not that it matters. I'm glad to do anything I can to help bring our Sophie back home, and I'm sure Dylan is, too."

"It's legal," Tom said. "But as a general rule, you don't have to talk to the police without a parent or guardian present."

"What is it you want to know?" Dylan turned to face Tom. "We've already told Detective Jarvis everything we know," he said, referring to Tom's chief investigator.

"I understand, but I have a couple of follow-up questions. Just trying to get the timeline straight in my head. I know this is difficult." He offered a sympathetic smile. "You dropped Sophie off around ten last night. Is that right?"

"Yes. She has a weekday curfew since she's been staying here." He flashed an enigmatic glance in Rae's direction.

"Where did you go during the evening?"

"Just drove around. Grabbed some burgers. Listened to music. Usual stuff." He shrugged.

"You didn't notice anything unusual when you

dropped her off? No strange cars parked on the street? Anything at all out of the ordinary?"

"Everything was normal."

"What about her behavior?"

He took a moment too long to answer. "She seemed fine."

"What about you, Hannah? When was the last time you talked to Sophie?"

"She texted last night after she got home. Nothing important. She had some questions about our chemistry assignment and I asked about her date."

"She didn't say anything to either one of you about going out to the Ruins?"

"Not to me. What about you, Dylan?"

He gave Hannah a frowning glance before he said, "No. But she's always had a thing about that place. She likes to take pictures out there. She once said the Ruins spoke to her. I didn't pay much attention. She's always been a little weird."

"That's why we love her," Hannah added.

"Kids don't still dare each other to go out there at night?" Tom asked.

"We can't speak for everyone in school," Hannah said. "But our group is a little more mature than that."

"What about you, Dylan? Were you ever dared to go out there?"

He looked uncomfortable. "Like Hannah said. We don't really do that sort of thing anymore."

"I've never thought Sophie the type to bend to peer pressure anyway," Rae said. "If anything, she's more of a ringleader. Or am I wrong about that?" She glanced from Dylan to Hannah and back to Tom. He had a hard time reading her expression at that moment. Did she suspect, as he did, that these two were holding out on them? Or did she take their earnest expressions at face value?

"Definitely a ringleader," Hannah agreed.

Tom caught an odd look on Dylan's face before he turned his attention back to the laptop.

"You mentioned a search party," Hannah said. "We have enough kids lined up to comb the whole area as soon as you give us the go-ahead. We'll take shifts and search all weekend if we have to." She turned to Rae. "If there is anything we can do for you, just name it. Sophie was like a sister to me. We've been best friends since first grade."

Tom's gaze sharpened at the girl's use of the past tense. An innocent mistake or something more sinister?

"Thank you both for your help," Rae said. "You've been wonderful. But if you'll excuse us, I need to have a word with Sheriff Brannon."

"Of course." Hannah smiled sweetly as she tucked back her straight brown hair. "We need to get to school anyway, but if it's okay, I'd like to check in with you later."

"Yes, I'm sure we'll talk again," Rae said with a brief nod.

She walked them to the door. When she came back into the kitchen, Tom stood at the window looking out over her backyard. He turned when he heard her footsteps, his gaze taking in her weary expression and the tired slump of her shoulders. She didn't look as if she'd slept a wink the night before. Tom could relate. He hadn't gotten any rest, either. Every time he closed his eyes, he saw too many bad things. He'd finally given up and gone back to the station.

"Coffee?" she asked.

"If it's not too much trouble."

She crossed the room and got down fresh mugs. "Cream and sugar?"

"Black is fine." She carried the cups over to the table and sat down. Tom came over and joined her. "Thanks," he said as he took a tentative sip. "This hits the spot. The coffee we have at the station tastes like feet."

She cradled her cup in both hands as if trying to absorb the warmth. "What did you make of those two?"

"What do you mean?"

She frowned. "They're hiding something. I may not have kids of my own, but it hasn't been that long since I was a teenager. The averted eyes. The cagey glances. Maybe I'm letting my imagination get the better of me, but I think they came over here to find out what I know."

"I don't think you're imagining things," Tom said slowly. "I think they're hiding something, too."

Her blue eyes deepened. "You don't suspect they had anything to do with Sophie's disappearance, do you? They're good kids, from what I know of them."

"Even good kids do bad things," Tom said. "At the very least, I think they knew Sophie was going to the Ruins and now they're too afraid to say so. I'll have them come down to the station separately to give statements. One of them is bound to crack. My guess is it'll be Dylan. Hannah is one cool cookie."

"Tracy Flick," Rae murmured.

Tom gave her a puzzled look. "Who?"

The barest hint of a smile flashed. "A movie reference. Never mind. What did you want to talk to me about?"

"I'd like to take a look at Sophie's room if that's okay."

"I've been through all the drawers and every square inch of her closet. And one of your deputies came and got her computer, so I doubt you'll find anything useful."

"You never know. Another pair of eyes," he said.

She drew a weary breath and stood. "I'll show you up."

The dark circles under her eyes against her pale complexion gave her a vulnerable air, a descriptor Tom would never have thought he'd apply to Rae Cavanaugh. She'd always seemed tough as nails. He hadn't realized how tiny she was, either. When he rose, she barely came to his shoulders. He supposed her commanding personality had always made her seem larger than life, but in the homey confines of her kitchen, she just looked small and scared and lost.

"Tom—"

"We're not even twenty-four hours in," he said. "We've still got time."

"Promise me you'll find her."

"I can't make that promise, but I swear to you I'll do everything in my power to bring her home safely."

Rae sighed. "I guess that will have to do."

TOM BRANNON DIDN'T wear a uniform. Rae wondered if that was because he wanted to set himself apart from the rest of the sheriff's department or if he desired to avoid the inevitable comparisons to his father. Porter Brannon had worn his khaki uniform with a great deal of flair. He'd been a tall man, like his son, and heavyset in his later years. A formidable figure in his Stetson and cowboy boots. Tom wore boots, too, but his were far less pretentious than the full-quill ostrich his father had favored. Nevertheless, his whole rustic, urban chic vibe—low-slung jeans, dark shirt and tie— worked for him. Worked for a lot of the women in town, too, Rae suspected.

Odd that she would be focusing on something as mundane as Tom Brannon's wardrobe when her niece was still missing. Maybe she was just trying to distract herself. Concentrate on something besides the phone call she'd made to Jackson in the wee hours of the morning. That call had been the second hardest thing she'd ever had to do. The first had been letting go of the notion that Riley would someday come home.

She paused outside Sophie's room, picturing her niece sprawled on the bed texting away on her cell phone. *Please, please, please let her be safe.*

"This is it," she said as she pushed open the door. She stood back for Tom to enter. The once sophisticated guest room had been made over into a girlie retreat. Band posters on the wall, photos taped to the dresser mirror, pink-and-white chenille spread on the bed. None of it was to Rae's taste and the clutter drove her crazy, but then, she wasn't fifteen anymore. Sometimes she wondered if she'd ever been that young. "Sophie has a fondness for pink," she said unnecessarily.

Tom glanced around. "I can see that. Reminds me a little of my sister's bedroom when we were kids."

The room was large and airy with a row of windows that let in plenty of natural light, but somehow Tom Brannon seemed to dominate the space, as only a tall, confident man could do. Rae wanted to resent him for the easy way he commanded his surroundings, but right now she just wanted him to find Sophie. If she had to pay tribute to the Brannons for the rest of her life, so be it.

"I talked to Jackson a few hours ago," she said. "He's on his way home. Fair warning—he'll be loaded for bear."

"A man's daughter goes missing, he has a right to be angry and scared."

"That's generous of you."

He gave her an inscrutable glance before he went back to his search. "You think I don't have compassion for what he's going through? You think my dad didn't have compassion for what your dad went through? It was a bad time for all of us," he said. "But your family suffered the most. No one in my family was unaware of that."

His words hit her like a physical punch. "I promised myself I wouldn't talk about that night. I wouldn't even think about it. This is a different time. Different girl, different situation. But what that man said last night." She paused with a shudder. "Do you think it's possible Preacher has come back?"

"I'm not even sure there ever was a Preacher," Tom said. "Silas Creed was a troubled man. Preacher was a fairy tale. A made-up bogeyman to keep kids away from the Ruins."

"For all the good that did. If he didn't take Riley and Jenna Malloy, then why did he leave town after they went missing? No one ever saw him after that night."

"My dad always figured Creed had someone in the area who helped him disappear. A relative, maybe. They probably knew he'd get blamed and felt sorry for him. Or maybe he really did take those girls. All I know is that whoever split open my skull that night had enough strength to drag me out of the Ruins and roll my body down the embankment."

"You were lucky you weren't killed," Rae said.

"You don't have to tell me how lucky I am. My sister, too. If I could go back and change the outcome—"

Rae turned away abruptly. She didn't want to hear Tom Brannon's regrets. She had enough of her own at the moment. "Why would Marty Booker say Preacher took Sophie if he didn't?"

"Marty Booker is also a troubled man," Tom said. "The description he gave of the abductor matched the face on the ceiling in the Ruins. He's confused at best. I'm not sure he even knows what he saw. His sister is coming in later to pick him up. Maybe she can get more out of him."

"You're just going to let him go?"

"For now. But don't worry. We'll keep an eye on him."

Rae dropped to the edge of the bed. "I wish there was more that I could do to find her. I feel like I should be out there beating the bushes with your deputies."

"Let them do their job right now. You're doing everything you can. Just try to relax."

"Easier said than done."

"I know that." He leaned in to examine the photos taped to the mirror. "Does Sophie keep a diary or journal?"

Rae traced a pattern on the bedspread. "I have no idea. But kids keep all that stuff online these days. Their whole lives are spread out all over social media. I can't even keep up with all the platforms."

"Do you know if she has accounts under different names?"

"No. But it wouldn't be unusual if she did. I have different accounts for business and personal use." Rae tracked him for a moment as he glanced behind the mirror and then tested the floorboards. "What are you doing?"

"Teenagers create hiding places for things they don't want others to find," he said.

"Sophie's been living under my roof for less than three weeks. You think she already ripped up the floorboards?"

"She had time to redecorate, didn't she? Kids her age are resourceful. I've seen it all."

Restless, Rae stood and walked over to the window to stare down at the garden. Despite the heat of late summer, the roses were still in bloom. She could almost smell the lush scent through the double-pane glass. She'd gotten her start from her mother's prized bushes, everything from American Beauties to Winter Sunsets. Rae didn't have her mother's green thumb. She was lucky to get a few decent blooms per season, but she was too stubborn to give up on the garden.

She said without turning, "Tell me about that night."

He didn't bother pretending to misunderstand. "You said you didn't want to talk about it or even think about it."

"I changed my mind."

"Wouldn't it be better if we focused on Sophie instead?" He sounded tired. And wary. Rae could hardly blame him, given their past.

She turned and leaned a shoulder against the window frame. "We are focusing on Sophie. I know it's a long shot to think the disappearances could be connected, but what if they are? What if Preacher really has come back to town? Anyway, I'd like to hear your version of that night."

He lifted a brow. "My version?"

She rested her head against the frame. "Your story. Your account. Call it whatever you like. I know you've told it before. Dozens of times, I'm sure, but I don't think I ever really listened. Why did you go out that night? Why did you leave the girls alone when you promised your folks you'd look after them?" She tried to keep her tone neutral, but a hint of accusation crept in. *Just tell me why.*

She wouldn't have been surprised if he had refused to answer, but he said in a resolved voice, "I drove out to that party to see a girl."

"Who?"

"Ashley Reardon. Do you remember her?"

Rae straightened from the window, conjuring the image of a pretty blonde cheerleader. "Ashley? Yes, I remember her. I never knew the two of you went out."

"We didn't. We were just starting to notice each other. After everything that happened that night..." He trailed away. "Whatever we had or could have had fizzled."

A lot of things had fizzled after that night. The world as Rae knew it had never been the same. She didn't know if Tom's candor made her feel better or worse. For as long as she could remember, she'd wanted to punish Tom Brannon and his family for failing to protect her sister. *His* sister had come home, after all. But how could she keep blaming Tom when she was the one who had really failed Riley? She was the one who was supposed to look out for her little sister. And now her niece had gone missing on Rae's watch. Payback had never tasted so bitter. Guilt had never felt darker or heavier than the curtain of regret that descended upon her shoulders.

"Ashley called that night and wanted to see me," Tom said. "I didn't want to say no, so I drove out to the party. We only talked for a few minutes. I was away from the house less than an hour, but when I got back, the girls were gone."

"How did you know where to look for them?"

"I called around and badgered my sister's friends until one of them told me about the dare. I drove straight to the bridge and ran all the way to the Ruins. By the time I got there, I was in a cold sweat. I knew that I would be in trouble if my parents found out, but I didn't care about the punishment. I had a bad feeling something was wrong the moment I set foot in that place."

Rae shivered. "And then you were ambushed."

"Another stupid mistake. I let down my guard."

"You were sixteen."

Their gazes connected for a moment before he

glanced away. "Nearly seventeen. And I was old enough to know better."

"Then what does that say about me? I was asleep when Sophie left the house. I didn't hear anything. I knew she had something on her mind when she came home earlier, but instead of trying to talk to her, I took the easy way out."

"You couldn't have known she'd leave the house."

"Neither could you."

Tom looked taken aback, but he couldn't have been any more stunned by her defense of him than she was. He'd been her enemy for fifteen years. A target for all her anguish and guilt. So why did she now feel the need to understand him? Why the desire to reach out to him, to draw comfort from his strength and resolve? Why did she wonder, all of a sudden, what it would be like to have his arms around her, holding her close as he murmured in her ear that all would be well?

She was just tired and worried and scared. She wasn't thinking straight. Hugging her arms around her middle, she looked anywhere but into Tom Brannon's troubled gray eyes.

He stirred restlessly. "I'm done in here."

Yes, so was Rae. She needed to be alone to regroup. Everything seemed strangely tilted in Sophie's room, as if the lingering emotions and confusion of a teenager had somehow infected Rae's common sense.

She led Tom back into the hallway and then turned to close the door. He was already at the top of the stairs when her phone rang. She fished her cell out of her jeans pocket and lifted it anxiously to her ear.

"Hello?"

"Rae, it's Dad. Don't say a word. Just listen. Something's happened. I need you to drop everything and get out to the ranch as quick as you can."

# Chapter Four

Rae clutched the phone. "Dad? What's going on?"

He paused for so long she thought he might have hung up. "Are you alone?"

She glanced at Tom, who waited on the landing.

"Sheriff Brannon is here," she tried to say without inflection.

Her father muttered an oath. "Get rid of him."

"He was just leaving. He came to search Sophie's room. No, we didn't find anything. Not yet." She shot Tom another look. "Try not to worry. I'll drive out as soon as I can."

"Get out here *now*." West Cavanaugh hung up without another word.

Tom watched her carefully. "Everything okay?"

She slipped the phone back into her pocket. "My father is having a difficult time, as you can imagine. Sophie's disappearance is bringing back a lot of painful memories. I need to go out to the ranch and be with him."

"I'd like to talk to him," Tom said. "To Jackson and his wife, too, as soon as they get back in town. Maybe I should drive out to the ranch with you."

Rae bit her lip. "Would you mind waiting until I have a chance to calm him down? I can usually get through to him if there aren't any distractions. He hasn't been in the best of health lately. He had a mild heart attack last winter."

"I didn't know that." Tom turned back to the stairs. "Are you sure everything is okay? Nothing else you want to talk to me about?"

"I've told you everything I know," Rae said. "I'm well aware that our best chance of getting Sophie back unharmed is to cooperate fully with your office."

"I'm glad to hear you say that."

They were in the foyer now, standing face-to-face. Tom stared down at her for the longest moment. He probably sensed something was up. Rae had never been that great of a poker player, but she couldn't exactly fill him in when she had no idea why her father had called. She resisted the urge to check the time on her phone. She needed to get out to the ranch. She needed to be there for her family. But Tom lingered.

"If you think of anything or hear of anything—"

"I'll call," she said as she reached around him

to open the door and then ushered him onto the porch. "You have my word."

Trailing him down the steps, she stood on the sidewalk and gave him a brief wave as he backed out of her driveway. She waited until his vehicle had disappeared around a corner before rushing back inside to grab her purse and car keys. Then she backed out of the garage, glanced both ways and laid down rubber as she wheeled into the street.

Fifteen minutes later, she pulled through the gateway arch that led to the Cavanaugh ranch. Speeding along the curving lane, she was oblivious to the pine trees and honeysuckle thickets that crowded the shoulder. Even with the sun shining down through the bowers, a perpetual gloom hovered, but she was used to all those shadows. She made the last corner and the trees thinned, allowing an expansive view of the rolling countryside. Light glinted off the pond where a mother duck and her babies skimmed across the surface and a heron fished in the shallows. In the distance, black cattle grazed peacefully against a backdrop of robin's egg blue.

The pastoral scene seemed obscenely incongruent with Sophie's disappearance, but the sight of the sprawling limestone-and-cedar house never failed to comfort Rae. Her happiest moments had been spent on the ranch. She and Jackson and

Riley riding horses on a frosty evening. Coming home to a crackling fire and the smell of baking bread and their mother's soft laughter as she bustled about the kitchen. Their father sipping whiskey in his recliner, a dog at his feet and a cat curled up on the hearth. Summers were even better. Waterskiing on the lake. Tubing on the river. Lounging on the back porch as thunderheads rolled in from the east.

After Rae's mother died, everything had gone to hell. Her father had eventually remarried and then divorced, Riley had disappeared and Rae and Jackson had grown so far apart she sometimes wondered if her brother actually hated her. If he didn't before, he certainly would now, she thought with dreaded certainty.

She pulled around to the back of the house and started to go in the kitchen entrance as she always did when she heard raised voices coming from the direction of her mother's rose garden. Stepping off the porch, she slipped unnoticed along the flagstone pathway. The French doors to her father's study were open, allowing in the morning breeze, and Rae paused to savor the garden before facing whatever terrible news waited for her inside.

As she stood there wrapped in the luscious scent of her mother's roses, she heard Jackson's voice lift in anger. So her brother was already back.

"How can you blame me for any of this? I wasn't even here!"

"Which is precisely why I hold you responsible," her father countered. "You're the girl's father, yet you had no qualms about pawning your only child off on your sister even though you know she has no experience in dealing with someone like Sophie."

"Someone like Sophie? What's that supposed to mean?"

"Do I have to spell it out for you?"

"She's a spirited girl," Jackson defended.

"She's a spoiled brat and you know it. That child has always needed a firm hand and a watchful eye. You've given her neither. And that wife of yours is no help. Although she does know how to spend money. I'll give her that."

"It's not enough to disparage my daughter, but now you have to set in on my wife?" Jackson grumbled bitterly. "Under the circumstances, I would have hoped for a little more understanding and compassion. The last thing I need is another lecture from you."

Her brother's sullen tone grated on Rae even as she berated herself for eavesdropping. She knew she should make her presence known, but she stood motionless in the garden, rooted by an indefinable worry. Why were they arguing about Jackson's second wife when his daughter had vanished from the Ruins just as Riley had? Didn't they understand that none of their petty grievances mattered anymore?

"I'm only telling you these things for your own good," West insisted. "When this is all over and Sophie is back home safe and sound, you need to take a long, hard look at yourself. You're nearly forty years old, Jackson. It's high time you grow up and take control of your life. You've made plenty of bad decisions in the past few months and the business has suffered as a result. You're away from the office at all hours. You drink too much, and you've allowed your wife to spend you to the verge of bankruptcy. I'm beginning to think I should have put Rae in charge."

"I'm surprised you didn't. She's always been your favorite." That sullen tone again. Rae winced.

"Your sister is a hard worker. She's earned my respect and devotion, and if I play favorites now and then, maybe it's because she's the spitting image of your mother. But you're my only son. I've always had high hopes for you. Maybe those expectations have been too much of a burden. I don't know. What I do know is that none of this matters a whit if we lose Sophie. Instead of worrying about Rae, you need to figure out how you're going to get your daughter back."

"How *I'm* going to get her back? Do you have any idea how cold you sound right now? She isn't just my daughter. She's your only grandchild. Or doesn't that mean anything to you?"

"Of course it means something to me. We're all in this together. Why do you think I asked Rae to come out here?"

"Where is she anyway? Shouldn't she be here by now?"

"She'll be here when she gets here," West said. "Stop that infernal pacing and try to relax."

"I need a drink," Jackson muttered.

"It's barely ten o'clock in the morning," West said reprovingly.

"Yes, and my daughter isn't home yet. If I want a whiskey, I'll damn well have one."

"Suit yourself."

Rae drew a breath and started to enter through the garden doors when a car sounded in the driveway. She retraced her steps around the house just as Lauren Cavanaugh exited her luxury sedan and strode up the walkway to the front entrance, using her key to let herself in. Rae went back around to the rear door and came in through the mudroom and kitchen, allowing her sister-in-law time to disappear down the hallway. The last thing she wanted was a confrontation with Jackson's wife. She'd never warmed up to the woman. Never really trusted her. But if Jackson was happy in his second marriage, then Rae's opinion didn't matter. As far as she could determine, no one in that household had been happy for a very long time, least of all Sophie.

Rae spoke to the housekeeper for a moment before heading down the long hallway to her father's study. Lauren was already seated on the leather sofa with her long legs crossed, revealing the red soles of her expensive heels. She wore a white dress belted at the waist and a gold-and-diamond bracelet around her wrist.

A former model, Lauren Cavanaugh was a tall, pale blonde with expensive tastes and a distant nature. She gave Rae's jeans and T-shirt a dismissive once-over as she accepted a mineral water from her husband. He sprawled on the sofa beside her, weary and anxious and yet somehow still defensive. Even under such distressing circumstances, the two made a striking couple. Rae's light brown hair and freckles came from her mother's side of the family while Jackson had inherited their father's height and dark good looks.

Rae went over and kissed her dad's cheek. As always, he smelled of fresh-cut grass with a hint of witch hazel. She drew in the scent, taking comfort in the familiar. The leather furniture, the paintings on the wall, all those well-loved books...

How she wished she could go back in time, to a point where Sophie was safe and sound and everything else was mundane. Maybe even further back so that she could see Riley one last time.

"I'm glad you're here, Rae." Her father patted her shoulder.

She straightened, her gaze moving from her father to her brother. The tension was as thick and choking as smoke. "I came as soon as I could. What's going on? Has there been news of Sophie?"

"Yes, we have news." West took her hand. "Brace yourself, honey. We've received a ransom demand."

AFTER LEAVING RAE'S HOUSE, Tom drove straight back to the station. The morning remained hot and sunny, and yet an eerie pall had settled over the town. Sophie Cavanaugh's disappearance had stirred a lot of bad memories in Belle Pointe. A lot of old fears and suspicions had been resurrected.

Tom wasn't immune. He'd been fighting a sense of déjà vu ever since Rae had reported her niece missing. He didn't want to believe Sophie's disappearance had anything to do with the incident fifteen years ago, but someone had picked the night of a blood moon to lure her to the Ruins. Surely not Preacher after all these years, but someone with knowledge of the past. Someone who knew the significance of the eclipse.

He itched to be out combing the countryside with his deputies. He felt powerless behind a desk, but if Sophie Cavanaugh didn't turn up soon, a million details would have to be coordinated. The investigation had to be done right. He couldn't afford to get careless.

Taking a momentary break, he leaned back in his chair and glanced outside. He could see the street from his desk. Traffic was light for a weekday morning. Little wonder. People who had heard the news would be staying close to home. Parents would want to keep an eye on their kids. Imagining themselves in a similar situation would strike cold terror in their hearts.

Tom's gaze lit on a solitary figure in the park across the street. Dylan Moody had been sitting on a bench in the shade of a pecan tree for the past ten minutes. He'd obviously ditched school. Maybe he just needed some time to himself, but the proximity of the park to the station led Tom to wonder if Sophie Cavanaugh's boyfriend was trying to work up the courage to come in. Tom thought about walking over and confronting him, but then he decided it might be better to let the boy stew for a while.

"Sheriff?"

He glanced up to find his civilian assistant hovering in the doorway. "What is it, Angie?"

She angled her head toward the squad room.

"You've got a visitor. Says his name is Blaine Fenton."

Tom glanced through the glass partition to the front of the building, where a dark-haired man paced nervously. He looked vaguely familiar, but Tom couldn't place him.

"Did he say what he wanted?"

Angie looked worried. "Says he needs to talk to you about the Cavanaugh girl."

"You'd better send him in, then." Tom turned back to the window. Dylan Moody was still out there, sitting hunched over as if he had a bad stomachache. *What are you hiding, kid?* What had him all torn up inside?

As if drawn by Tom's scrutiny, Dylan glanced across the street at the station. His gaze moved over the brick facade before coming to rest— Tom could have sworn—on his office window. The boy sat transfixed for the longest moment before he finally got up and hurried away, casting a worried look over his shoulder before he disappeared into the trees.

A shadow appeared in the doorway and Tom tore his gaze from the park.

The man hovered on the threshold, shuffling his feet as he ran a finger around the brim of his Stetson.

*He's nervous*, Tom thought. "Blaine Fenton?"

The man cleared his throat. "Thank you for agreeing to see me, Sheriff."

Tom swiveled his chair around and leaned an elbow on his desk. "How can I help you?"

"I'm hoping I can help you."

Tom sized him up. "You know something about Sophie Cavanaugh's disappearance?"

"Not directly. But I know something."

"That's plenty vague. Everybody knows something." Tom straightened and motioned to the chair across from his desk. "Maybe you'd better sit down and tell me what's on your mind."

The man took a seat and placed his hat on the floor beside his chair. He looked to be in his late thirties, tall and fit with the air of a man accustomed to hard work. He wore jeans, boots and a plaid shirt with pearl snaps up the front. Ordinary attire for Nance County.

"You may not know this, but our dads used to be friends," he said. "Pop always spoke highly of the sheriff. He said Porter Brannon was one of the finest men he ever knew."

"That's always nice to hear," Tom said. "What's your dad's name?"

"Bill Fenton. He owns a small ranch north of here. Part of his property borders the Cavanaugh spread. We're small potatoes by comparison, but we always got on well with the family. Jackson and I played baseball together when we were kids and I used to ride horses with Rae. Sometimes Riley would tag along. Real sweet kid. Shame what happened to her."

"Yes, it is."

The man's thoughts seemed to drift for a moment before he reined in his focus. "After I left the military, I worked for the Cavanaughs for a time."

"I get it," Tom said. "You go back a long way with the family."

Blaine Fenton nodded. "About two years ago, Pop got bad sick. Lung cancer. No insurance. The medical bills piled up quick. He went to West Cavanaugh and offered to sell him the water rights to a parcel of land the family had been trying to buy for years. Cavanaugh had the papers drawn up and my dad signed them. It wasn't until they started moving heavy drilling equipment onto the land that Pop realized he'd also signed away the oil and gas rights. This happened just months before the discovery became public of the new natural gas deposits in the Haynesville-Bossier Shale."

Tom gave him a long scrutiny. "You think West Cavanaugh knew about the discovery before he signed those papers?"

"Of course he knew." Bitterness crept into Blaine Fenton's voice. "Why else would he have slipped that clause into the contracts?"

"Didn't your dad have an attorney look over the paperwork before he signed?"

Fenton's lips thinned as his tone sharpened. "Yes. An attorney recommended by West Cavanaugh. You have to consider how sick Pop was back then. Between the chemo and radiation, he wasn't thinking clearly, and the Cavanaughs took advantage of his frailty."

"Where were you during this time?"

A look flashed across the man's face that Tom couldn't name. Could have been guilt. Could have been annoyance at a perceived implication. "I'd been living out west for a few years. I came home as soon as I found out about Pop's illness."

Tom fiddled with a pen on his desk. "Sounds like your family has had a rough go of it and I'm sorry about that. But what does any of this have to do with Sophie Cavanaugh's disappearance?"

"I'm getting to that." Outwardly, Fenton's nerves appeared to be under control, but beneath his calm surface, he was still a man on edge. "After I found out what happened, I hired an attorney willing to take our case on contingency. She's believed all along that we have a good chance in court. Folks around here don't appreciate anyone taking advantage of the elderly. Or anyone swindling a sick man out of hundreds of thousands of dollars by one of their neighbors.

Having public opinion on our side means a sympathetic jury pool."

"Still waiting for your point," Tom said.

Fenton leaned in. "After more than a year of delays and mediation, the case is set to go to trial next month. Just weeks away from the court date and Sophie Cavanaugh disappears, reminding people of what happened to West Cavanaugh's youngest daughter. All of a sudden, sympathy shifts to his side."

"Let me see if I follow," Tom said slowly. "You think West Cavanaugh had his own granddaughter abducted in order to sway public opinion?"

"Yes. That's exactly what I think. Don't get me wrong. I'm not suggesting he'd have the girl harmed. She's probably stashed away in some fancy spa or maybe out on the ranch somewhere. She'll turn up in a few days none the worse for the wear. The family will keep her out of the public eye until after the trial so that imaginations can run wild. In the meantime, they'll use all their resources, including their kin at the *Echo Lake Star*, to smear my dad and challenge his mental state. People forget that the Cavanaughs have a stake in the local paper, so they don't always see the bias."

"Maybe you're not giving people around here enough credit. And maybe you're placing too much importance on a small-town weekly," Tom said. "No one relies on local newspapers any-more."

"People who serve on juries do."

Tom allowed that he might have a point.

Blaine Fenton scowled across the desk. "Think about how they used to go after your dad. Sher-iff Brannon could never catch a break. Nothing he did was ever good enough. That paper ham-mered him for years and you know damn well West Cavanaugh was behind those attacks. I al-ways tried to give the old man a break for his bit-terness. Losing a child like that..." He shook his head. "But now I think he went after your dad because Porter Brannon couldn't be bought. And the Cavanaughs will do the same thing to you if you don't watch your back."

Tom thought about all the nasty rumors and innuendos that had been launched by his polit-ical opponent and the heated rhetoric that had been sanctioned on the editorial pages of the *Echo Lake Star*. All through that campaign, Tom had had to remind himself that politics was a dirty business and he couldn't allow himself to take any of it personally. But he was only human. The attack on his character had stung. He knew firsthand how brutal the Cavanaughs could be when they viewed you as the enemy. Even so, he didn't want to attach too much credence to Blaine Fenton's theory. The man obviously harbored a grudge and everything he said had to be filtered through that lens. Yet a seed of doubt had been planted.

"It's an interesting theory," Tom said. "But that's all it is. Not much I can do without hard evidence."

"You can keep an open mind," Fenton said. "That's all I'm asking."

Tom sat back in his chair. "Are you sure you aren't trying to stir up trouble because of an old grudge?"

"I'm not stirring up anything. I haven't said a word to anyone else about my concerns. But it's been on my mind ever since I heard about the girl's disappearance. I figured I needed to come in and say my piece. Whatever happens now is out of my hands." He picked up his hat and stood. "Thank you for your time, Sheriff."

Tom rose, too. "Leave your contact information with my assistant in case I need to get in touch with you."

Fenton hesitated. "I don't know why you would. I've told you everything I know. I'd as soon my name is kept out of it. People might assume as you did that I have an ax to grind." He paused as another frown flashed. "Just don't make the mistake of underestimating West Cavanaugh. He's done a lot of good in Nance County, fooled a lot of people, but my father learned the hard way that he's as ruthless as they come. And from what I can tell, the apple doesn't fall far from the tree."

Tom leaned a hip against the corner of his desk. "Are you now suggesting Jackson Cavanaugh had something to do with his daughter's disappearance?"

"I wasn't talking about Jackson."

The insinuation blindsided Tom, though he wasn't sure why. "You think Rae Cavanaugh is somehow involved?"

Fenton said grimly, "Put it this way, Sheriff. Jackson doesn't have the smarts or the stomach to pull off something like this. I grew up with those kids, and in my experience, people don't change that much. Riley was the sweet one, Jackson was the hothead and Rae was always one step ahead of everyone else."

Rae was smart, no question, but Tom couldn't imagine her having anything to do with her niece's disappearance. She'd been genuinely distressed when she called last night and even more so this morning. Or was she that good of an actress?

Fenton gave him a knowing look. "Don't let that pretty smile fool you, Sheriff. Way down deep, Rae Cavanaugh's every bit as cunning as her old man."

# Chapter Five

Rae stared at her father in stunned disbelief. A ransom demand had never entered her mind. She supposed she'd subconsciously melded Sophie's disappearance with Riley's. In her sister's case, there had never been any communication with the abductor, much less a final resolution. The day Riley went missing had started out as any other and then she was just…gone.

But a ransom demand implied that Sophie could still be alive.

Tears flooded Rae's eyes, but she blinked them away and tried to remain resolute. Kidnappings for ransom didn't always turn out well, either. So many things could go wrong. But Sophie had been gone for less than a day. Tom Brannon said they still had time. Rae clung to that.

"When? *How?* What are the demands?"

"The call came in on the landline just before Jackson arrived," West said. "I was here alone. The caller used one of those electronic gizmos to disguise his voice. I couldn't tell if I was speaking to a man or a woman. Whoever called demanded a cool million in twenty-four hours for Sophie's safe return."

Rae's stomach knotted with dread. "How do we know it isn't a hoax? Maybe someone heard about Sophie's disappearance and is trying to cash in."

"We don't know," West said. "Not yet. We've only had the one call."

Rae took a moment to calm her thudding heart. "Twenty-four hours isn't much time to raise that kind of cash."

"But you can do it, right?" Lauren had been silent since Rae arrived. Now she rose and went over to West's desk, placing her palms on the surface as she leaned in anxiously. "You can get the money. It isn't that much, really. Not by Cavanaugh standards."

"A million dollars is a great deal of money by anyone's standards," West snapped. "Contrary to what you seem to think, money doesn't grow on trees around here."

"Dad, please," Jackson pleaded.

"Please what?" West demanded.

Lauren whirled to face Rae, her eyes clouded with anguish. Rae had never seen her sister-in-law's facade slip, but something that might have been fear clawed its way up to that cool, placid surface. "There must be something you can do. Holdings that you can liquidate. Lines of credit that you can tap into. Don't tell me there isn't a way!"

"Let's just try to stay calm." Rae was scared, too, but she deliberately kept her tone even. "I'll talk to the bank if that's how we want to play it. We should also call Sheriff Brannon. He needs to know about this."

"No cops." West was blunt and adamant. "The son of a bitch said he'd kill Sophie if we involve the authorities."

Lauren gasped. Jackson swore. A cold chill shot through Rae.

West pressed home his point. "We've got to be smart about this. Porter Brannon never did a damn thing to bring Riley home. I'm not about to put Sophie's life in the hands of his son."

"I don't think that's fair," Rae said. "Tom isn't his father."

Three pairs of eyes stared her down. No one said anything for a long, tense moment and then her father's gaze narrowed. "What did you say?"

Rae wavered in the face of her father's hostility, but she didn't back down. "Just because Porter Brannon couldn't find Riley doesn't mean Tom won't find Sophie."

Jackson stepped forward, fists clenched at his sides. "I can't believe what I'm hearing. What is wrong with you? Don't you remember anything about the night our little sister went missing? Tom was supposed to be watching those girls, but instead he left them alone while he went out partying. What happened to Riley was his fault."

Rae took a breath. "Then what happened to Sophie is my fault."

She hadn't really expected Jackson to leap to her defense, but the white-hot fury in his eyes shook her to the core. "Damn right it's your fault. If anything happens to my daughter, I will never forgive you."

"That's enough," West said. "It doesn't help Sophie if we turn on each other. We need to keep our heads on straight, so we don't make any stupid mistakes."

"I'm sorry," Rae said.

Jackson turned away with a shrug.

Rae dropped down onto an armchair. She'd been bracing for the confrontation with her brother ever since she'd discovered Sophie missing from her room, but nothing could have truly prepared her for Jackson's scorn. She told herself he was just scared. Even without the history of a missing sister, any parent would be terrified in his place. But Riley had to be on his mind. She was on everyone's mind. If he needed to take his fears out on Rae, then so be it.

But there was something about his behavior

that struck a wrong note. Yes, he was scared, but he also seemed jittery, as if he'd mainlined a gallon of black coffee. He couldn't be still. He sat down on the sofa only to pop back up a moment later to pace to the window. Lauren watched with hooded eyes, her gaze keen and calculating. For whatever reason, Rae's mind went back over the accounting discrepancies she'd found recently. Invoices from companies she couldn't track down. Cattle bought and sold without proper documentation. She didn't like where her thoughts were headed, so she forced her attention back to her father. He sat back down at his desk and stared at the phone as if he could somehow will it to ring.

"Dad?"

He glanced up with a frown. "What?"

"If you don't trust the county sheriff's office, what about calling the FBI? They know how to handle kidnappings."

He glared at her. "Did the feds find Riley?"

"They were called in late—"

"Yes, and I remember the guy they finally sent down here." He gave a derisive snort. "Fresh out of Quantico. Green behind the ears. About as useful as any of Porter Brannon's idiot deputies."

"I just think—"

Jackson had been pacing in front of the window, but now he stormed over to her chair and got in her face. "Enough, Rae! No cops means *no cops*. Local, federal or otherwise. You heard what Dad said. This time we take care of things our way."

Rae put up a hand warning her brother to back off. "Our way? What does that even mean?"

"It means we get on the same page right this very minute." West's gaze swept the study with steely resolve. "Nothing we say leaves this room. Are we clear on that?"

"I understand how you feel," Rae said. "But even if we come up with the ransom, there's no guarantee they'll let Sophie go. We need backup. We're taking an awfully big risk not bringing in the authorities."

Jackson gave her another contemptuous glance. He'd retreated a few steps, but he still hovered. "Don't cross us on this, Rae. You always think you know better than anyone else, but this is not your decision to make. You've already done enough without going behind our backs to the cops."

"I'm not going behind your back. Since when am I not entitled to an opinion?"

West leaned forward. "Do you trust me? Forget this ridiculous feud with your brother. Do you trust *me*?"

She sighed. "Of course I trust you, Dad."

"Then believe me when I tell you we'd be taking a far bigger risk by calling in the authorities.

For all we know, someone could be watching the ranch at this very moment. They may even have planted surveillance inside the house. If we call the cops, they'll know it."

"They?"

"I got the impression more than one person is involved in this thing. It's likely we're dealing with professionals."

Her father was starting to sound paranoid, but Rae couldn't help glancing around the room with another shudder. Jackson was back at the window staring out at the garden. He'd distanced himself from the conversation, but Lauren clung to every word. She seemed fascinated by the back-and-forth.

"Something you want to add?" Rae couldn't help asking.

"What's there to add? West is absolutely right. It would be a mistake to bring in the police."

He spared her a withering glance. There had never been any love lost between West Cavanaugh and his daughter-in-law, so he wasn't likely to be swayed by her truckle. After a moment, he dropped his gaze back to the phone in dismissal. "If we want Sophie back alive, we have to do exactly as the kidnappers say. We have to trust that all they want is money. But I won't give them one red cent until they provide proof of life."

"When should we expect another call?" Rae asked nervously.

"I don't know. I was told to stay close to the phone."

She nodded. "Then I'll handle the financial arrangements. Jackson can stay here with you."

"I've already phoned Glen Stafford," West said, referring to their longtime banker. "I didn't give him specifics and he didn't ask for any. We've done business long enough that my word is good enough for him. All you need to do is go down to the bank in a few hours, sign the papers and bring the money straight back here."

"A few hours? How is that possible? First National is a small bank," Rae said. "They don't have that kind of cash on hand, do they?"

"Leave the details to Glen. He said he'd have the money. He'll have the money."

Jackson turned from the window. "If you already had it worked out with the bank, then why didn't you say so? Why put me through hell with all that talk about getting my house in order? You couldn't have waited until we have Sophie back to tear into me?"

"I told you some hard truths," West said. "When this is all over, we're going to make some changes around here, starting with you two." He pointed a finger at first Jackson and then Lauren. She stiffened, but didn't turn away. "No more expensive trips, no more shopping sprees, no more anything until you work yourselves out of debt. As for you." He turned to Rae. "I've always had complete faith in your judgment, but if you're going soft on Tom Brannon, I may have to rethink my position."

She frowned. "I'm not going soft. I'm just trying to be fair."

"Was it fair that Porter Brannon's daughter came home and mine didn't? Was it fair that his son left those young girls alone in the house that night? Nothing about this situation is fair, Rae. Keep your head on straight and let's just get through this. We'll deal with Tom Brannon later."

"Sheriff?"

Tom turned to find Angie back at his door, this time with her purse hooked over her shoulder.

"Going somewhere?" he asked.

"It's Friday noon. I'm out of here until Monday morning."

"Is it that late already?" He glanced at his watch. The hours had flown by.

"Boy Wonder's in the back," she said, referring to Noah Goodnight. "He says he's found something on Sophie's phone that you should take a look at."

Tom nodded. "I'm headed that way now. You have a good weekend."

"You sure you don't want me to stay?"

"I'll call you back in if I need you. Otherwise, go home and relax."

"Thanks. I intend to. You try to get some rest, too. You've been up all night and half the day. You look like hell," she said in her usual direct manner.

"I feel that way, too." Tom followed her out into the squad room and they parted ways as he headed down the hallway to the back of the building to find his deputy.

A graduate of Sam Houston University with dual degrees in criminal justice and forensic studies, Noah Goodnight was one of Tom's most successful recruits. Tom was under no illusion that a deputy of Noah's caliber would remain in a place like Belle Pointe forever. He'd eventually get bored and move on to greener pastures, most likely to a midsize city like Tyler at first and then to Dallas or Fort Worth. Tom would never be able to match the incentives or salary of a big-city police department, but for as long as Noah remained in Nance County, Tom intended to take full advantage of the man's skills.

He pushed open the door and nodded to both Noah and Craig Jarvis, the senior detective in Criminal Investigations. Craig was a twenty-year veteran on the force. He wasn't flashy or cocky like some of the younger officers. He preferred

the background to the limelight, and his hunched
shoulders and easygoing demeanor could sometimes be mistaken for a man cruising toward re-
tirement. He and Tom had been partners early
in Tom's career, and he'd quickly learned that
beneath Craig's low-key exterior lurked a clever
and determined investigator. He had been the first
to encourage Tom to run for his dad's old office,
the first to congratulate him when he won and
the first to stand shoulder to shoulder with him
when resentment had reared its ugly head in the
department.

Tom pulled up a stool and sat down at a counter across from Noah. "You've got something for
me?"

The young deputy gave him a brief nod. "Two
things. The blood analysis came back from the
sample that was collected last night at the Ruins.
It's not a match for Sophie Cavanaugh or Marty
Booker."

"So we have conclusive proof a third person
was in that building last night," Tom said.

"It's not a match for Silas Creed, either, for
whatever that's worth," Craig added.

"No big surprise there," Tom said. "But it's always good to eliminate every possibility, no matter how slight. What else?"

The younger officer held up the pink encased
cell phone Tom had found in the boiler room.

"I've been going through Sophie's text messages. It's mostly just high school stuff, but I came across a series of group texts that could be important."

"I'm all ears," Tom said.

"There are four people texting back and forth in this particular group, including Sophie, Dylan Moody and Hannah Tucker. I haven't been able to trace the fourth number to anyone in Sophie's contacts. They've all replaced the letters in their names with symbols. See?" He turned the screen so they could take a look. "Those kids have been going out to the Ruins for weeks. I think they're involved in some sort of game."

"I saw Hannah and Dylan at Rae Cavanaugh's house this morning," Tom said. "They told me flat out they didn't go out to the Ruins anymore and had no idea why Sophie would have gone there alone."

"They told me the same thing," Craig said.

Noah shrugged. "Kids lie all the time. Question is, why are these two lying?"

"What do you think these symbols mean?" Tom asked.

"Think of them as Monopoly pieces. Each player has a unique token. Remember the photos of the Ruins that Rae Cavanaugh found on Sophie's laptop? When I blew up the images, I found these same symbols on some of the walls inside the building." He turned the laptop around so that Tom and Craig could scrutinize the images.

Tom leaned in to get a better look.

"From what I can piece together from the texts, the rules of the game are pretty simple," Noah said. "The first player enters the Ruins, probably at night, to hide his or her symbol somewhere inside the building. On a wall, on the floor, the ceiling, wherever. The second player arrives on a different night with the objective of finding the first player's symbol. Player Number Two then hides his or her symbol elsewhere so that the third player has to find both. They go deeper into the building with each trip and the game becomes riskier. The more symbols a player finds, the more points he or she is awarded. It's kind of like a scavenger hunt."

"A creepy scavenger hunt, if you ask me," Craig muttered.

"That's not even the creepiest part," Noah said. "The symbols seem to represent people who were connected to the disappearances of those girls fifteen years ago."

"You're right. That is creepier."

"Connected how?" Tom asked.

"Sophie's symbol is a gemstone—a Riley. Dylan Moody uses a six-point star." Noah pointed to the badge clipped to Tom's belt. "Your father was sheriff back then. The star probably represents your sister or you or maybe even your whole family. Hannah Tucker uses a lightning bolt. That one took me a while to figure out. Then I remembered that the girl who was found wandering on the side of the road—Jenna Malloy—was in and out of psychiatric hospitals for years. The lightning bolt is probably meant to represent electroshock therapy. The fourth player uses a cross."

Tom felt a chill along his spine. "Preacher?"

Craig gave a low whistle. "Now Booker's account is starting to make sense. When he told you that Preacher had taken Sophie, we assumed in his confusion he meant Silas Creed. But what if he saw *this* Preacher?"

Tom nodded. "He also said, 'I see them, but they don't see me.' I assume he meant the players." He turned back to Noah. "So the fourth player—Preacher—is the number you haven't been able to track down."

"I tried calling and texting. Nothing. No voice mail or anything. I figure it's a burner that got tossed after the prepaid minutes were used up. We can trace the number back to the point of purchase, but that takes time and it still may not tell us who bought the phone."

Tom glanced at Craig. "Is Marty Booker still in lockup?"

"His sister picked him up a little while ago."

"We'll need to bring him in again. Or better

yet, see if you can talk to him at his sister's house. He may feel less threatened in a friendly environment. We'll need to bring in Hannah Tucker and Dylan Moody, too. Call their parents and get them to agree to a time. Let's do this by the book."

"I'm on it."

"Any objection to me running out to the Ruins and taking a look at these symbols in person?" Noah asked. "I don't think there's much else to be found on Sophie's phone."

"Go ahead." Tom pushed the stool up under the counter. "Both of you keep me posted. I'm on my way out to the Cavanaugh ranch. Sophie's parents should be back in town by now. I'll see if they know anything about this game. At the very least, maybe they can tell me if Sophie has made any new friends recently."

Craig stuffed his notebook into his pocket. "Does it seem strange to anyone but me that none of the Cavanaughs have been by the station this morning? They're not exactly shrinking violets. You'd think they'd want an update on the investigation. If it were my daughter or granddaughter, I'd be camping out on your doorstep."

"A lot of things about this case are strange," Tom said.

# Chapter Six

Rae picked up the money at the bank after lunch and then left through Glen Stafford's private entrance to avoid curious stares. She didn't ask how he'd managed to come up with the cash so quickly. She was just grateful *he* didn't ask questions.

Storing the bag in the back seat of her SUV, she eased around the building and pulled onto the street. She tried to remain calm and alert, but she felt as if a big target had been painted on her back. All the way home she kept an eye on the rearview mirror. Even though she didn't see any suspicious vehicles behind her, she didn't rule out the possibility of a tail. For all she knew, she could have been followed from the moment she left the ranch.

Gripping the steering wheel, she shifted her focus to the road ahead of her. The county highway had plenty of cutoffs and wooded areas where someone could lie in wait. She was starting to feel a little paranoid, but if her dad's hunch was right, the whole family could be under surveillance.

Turning off the main road, she breathed a sigh of relief as she drove through the metal archway. She felt safer now that she was on her home turf, but she didn't let down her guard until the house was in sight. Even then, her reprieve was short-lived. A full-size SUV sped up the driveway toward her. Panic welled until she spotted the lights across the top of the cab. She couldn't see the driver or the emblem on the door, but she knew the visitor was Tom Brannon.

Rae bit her lip, wondering if she should pretend she didn't see him and take the money inside or if she should wait for him beside her vehicle. Might be a good idea to speak to him first before he talked to the others. She could at least find out what he wanted. If he had news of Sophie, then she would be able to prepare her family.

She got out and locked the doors, then lifted a hand to shield her eyes from the sun as she watched the vehicle's approach. The day was hot and humid. She could feel dampness gathering between her shoulder blades, but the perspiration was more from nerves than heat. She pulled the T-shirt away from her skin and tried to assume a poised demeanor as she waited for the big SUV to circle the driveway.

Tom Brannon got out and strode toward her, tall and formidable, a man on a mission. His cuffs were rolled back, and he'd loosened his collar and tie in the heat. He might have been anyone from a businessman to a cowboy save for the glint of his badge and the gun at his hip.

Rae took a step toward him. "Tom? What are you doing here? What's happened? Have you found Sophie?"

"No, it's nothing like that."

"Thank goodness." She drew a sharp breath. "That came out wrong. I don't mean I'm thankful you haven't found her. It's just—"

"I know what you meant." He walked over to where she waited beside her car. Her heart skipped a beat when he glanced through the tinted windows. The bag sat on the back seat, in plain sight if he peered closely enough. "It's a difficult time for your family."

"You've no idea." She shifted her position, drawing his attention away from her vehicle.

He stared across the space between them, peering into her eyes instead of through the car window. The effect did nothing to ease Rae's disquiet. She could see herself mirrored in his sunglasses. She looked pale and anxious and not altogether trustworthy. Abruptly, she turned away.

Tom said, "I told you earlier I need to talk to

the rest of the family. I never heard back from you about a time."

"I'm sorry. I meant to let you know. I'm not thinking too clearly right now."

He nodded. "No problem. I saw you in town just now. I tried to flag you down, but I guess you didn't see me."

She turned back to him in distress. "You saw me in town? Where?"

"You were pulling onto the highway. I figured you were on your way to the ranch."

"You followed me?"

"I was headed out here anyway." He took off his sunglasses and tucked them into his shirt pocket. "Is your brother back yet?"

The question *sounded* routine, yet Rae detected a subtle note of annoyance—or was that suspicion?—in his voice. She tried to swallow past her anxiety, but the steadiness of his gaze sent a ripple of awareness along her spine. Tom Brannon was nobody's fool. He could tell from her behavior that something was wrong. He would give her some leeway because of the situation, but that would go only so far before he started picking apart her body language.

With an effort, she looked him in the eyes without flinching, focusing on the attractive crinkles at the corners rather than the depth of his gaze. "He and Lauren both got in a little while ago."

Tom glanced away, turning his attention to the wooded drive and the highway beyond for a moment. His silence seemed ominous.

"What aren't you telling me?" Rae demanded.

His gaze came back to her. "There've been some new developments in the case."

She tried to remain calm, but her heart pummeled her chest. "What new developments? Tell me if I need to prepare myself."

His gaze softened. "We haven't found Sophie, but we do have some new information. For one thing, the blood we found at the Ruins last night isn't a match for Sophie or Marty Booker. We now know for certain a third person was in the building last night."

"But we already knew that." Rae rubbed the back of her arm, hoping he wouldn't notice the chill bumps popping on her skin or the tremor in her fingers. "You and I talked about it this morning. Marty Booker said that Preacher took Sophie."

"The blood isn't a match for Silas Creed, either," he said. "We can eliminate that possibility."

"You never believed he'd come back anyway."

"No."

"But he could still be alive."

"It's possible," Tom said. "My guess is he's long dead."

Rae glanced out over the property, frowning

into the sunlight. Was someone out there right now watching them, taking note of her interaction with the sheriff? Would they punish Sophie if anyone in the family made a wrong move? She closed her eyes on a shiver. "So we still don't know who took my niece. With each passing moment she could be slipping farther away from us."

"You can't lose hope," Tom said. "It's early yet, and like I said, we have new information that could turn into a significant lead. Can we go inside? It'll save time if I explain everything to all of you at once."

Rae hesitated, keenly aware of all that money on the back seat. The doors were locked and the vehicle in plain view of the house, but that was a lot of cash to leave lying around. Still, she couldn't very well open the door and remove the bag without arousing Tom's suspicions.

She wasn't overly trusting of law enforcement, particularly after their failure to find her sister. Despite that, her instinct was to come clean with Tom. She wanted desperately to trust him, but he was a Brannon and she was a Cavanaugh. Fifteen years of misgiving and animosity didn't disappear overnight. And anyway, her brother was right. It wasn't her call. She'd already made one bad mistake. Sophie had gone missing on her watch. What if she went behind Jackson's back and told Tom about the ransom demand? What if the kidnappers really were watching? What if they hurt Sophie because Rae hadn't followed their orders? She'd never be able to live with herself.

But what if they hurt Sophie anyway? What if this whole thing blew up in their faces? Could she live with herself then?

Doubts churned as she opened the front door and motioned Tom inside. The living space had been remodeled a few years ago into a wide-open concept. The foyer led into a spacious family room with plank flooring and a beamed ceiling. Rae could see all the way through the dining room into the kitchen. Lauren stood at the island pouring a glass of wine. She glanced up when she heard the front door. She walked around the island and came through the dining room into the family room.

"Rae? What took you so long—" She broke off when she spotted Tom in the foyer. Then her gaze darted back to Rae. "You didn't—"

"Forget to call Sheriff Brannon? I'm afraid I did." Rae gave her a warning look. "He tried to flag me down in town, but I didn't see him. So he drove all the way out here to speak to the family. There've been some new developments in the case."

Something flickered at the back of Lauren's eyes. "What new developments? Is Sophie—"

"She hasn't been found yet," Rae said. "Let's

just go into the study. Is Jackson still in there with Dad?"

"Yes, but I wish you'd tell me what's going on."

"I've told you everything I know. Sheriff Brannon will fill us in on the rest. Oh, and I'd advise you to leave the wine." She nodded to the stemware in Lauren's hand. "You know how Dad disapproves of imbibing before five, much less before lunch." She made a point of glancing at her watch even though she already knew the hour. Why she felt the need to antagonize her sister-in-law at a time like this, Rae couldn't say. Maybe it was because Lauren had never really given Sophie a chance and Rae felt defensive and resentful on her niece's behalf. Maybe it was because both Lauren and Jackson had leaped at the chance to dump their responsibilities so that they could take off for sunnier ports.

Or maybe she just wasn't a very nice person, Rae acknowledged.

Lauren polished off the wine and gave her a defiant glare as she set the glass on a nearby side table instead of returning it to the kitchen. Tom hadn't said a word during the whole confrontation. He hovered in the doorway waiting for his cue.

"This way," Rae said and turned on her heel.

They walked down the hallway together and Rae knocked sharply before opening the double doors. Her brother and dad looked up expectantly. Their gazes lit on Tom, but before they could utter a protest, Rae said, "Sheriff Brannon needs a word."

Her father was seated behind his desk while Jackson stood silhouetted against the French doors. He stood frozen, his gaze going from Rae to Tom and finally to Lauren. She walked around Rae and took her usual place on the sofa. No one said anything for the longest moment. It was as if the presence of a Brannon in West Cavanaugh's inner sanctum had rendered them all speechless.

Then Jackson's surly nature rallied. He came forward, his expression both puzzled and hostile. "Rae? What's going on?"

"Tom needs to talk to you about Sophie. I'm sure he has a lot of questions for all of us. He is the sheriff, you know."

"That fact hasn't escaped any of us."

"Try to keep a civil tongue." She gave her brother the same warning glance she'd shot Lauren earlier. "We need to hear what he has to say."

West sat forward. "Have you found my granddaughter yet?"

"No, sir, I'm afraid not. But we do have a promising lead." Tom came all the way into the room then, commanding the attention of even his enemies. Rae had to admire his professional aplomb. The simmering aggression in the study was butter-thick and razor-sharp, but Tom's tone was all business. He told them about the blood analysis first and how it disputed Marty Booker's claim that Preacher had taken Sophie. Then he launched into a lengthier explanation about the text messages and symbols found on Sophie's phone and how they seemed to relate to the pictures of the Ruins that were on her computer. When he finished, they all stared at him with a mixture of incredulity and anxiety.

Rae hardly knew what to make of any of it. "Sophie was playing a game?"

Tom nodded. "The best we can tell, she and her friends have been playing for weeks."

Jackson looked beside himself. Every muscle in his body tensed as he balled his hands into fists at his sides. "That's it? That's the promising lead?"

"It's more than we had this morning," Tom said.

Jackson shook his head as if he, too, were trying to make sense of it all. "You found some text messages on my daughter's phone and now you think someone kidnapped her because of a stupid game?"

"We think the game may have been used as a ruse to lure Sophie to the Ruins alone."

"But you said she and her friends have been playing the game for weeks," Rae said. "Why wait until last night to take her?"

Tom shrugged. "Could have been a matter of

timing and circumstances. Or the suspect may have had to work up his nerve. We just don't know."

"*His* nerve?" Rae asked.

"If Sophie was abducted, the suspect is most likely male, but we're not ruling out any possibility at this point." Tom turned back to Jackson. "Has Sophie talked about any new acquaintances lately? Have you seen her with anyone outside her ordinary circle of friends?"

Jackson remained brusque and uncooperative. "You'd have to ask my sister. Sophie has been staying with her for the past three weeks."

Rae winced. The accusation in his voice was like the point of a dagger in her heart. Guilt made her a tender target. Maybe that was why she'd felt the need to goad her sister-in-law. Just like after Riley's disappearance, Rae found it easier to blame and deflect than to examine too closely her own culpability.

If she were honest with herself, she'd have to admit that she hadn't exactly been Sophie's champion. Rae had been too caught up in her own life. She'd never taken the time to get to know her niece like she should have. Would it have killed her to take Sophie shopping or to a movie now and then? Was it that much of an inconvenience to sit down and have a heart-to-heart with the girl? What if it was too late to do any of those things now? What if Rae never got the chance to tell Sophie how much she cared about her? What if she never got the chance to say goodbye?

At the back of her mind, Riley materialized, but only for a moment before she melted back into the misty unknown. Tears welled in Rae's eyes, but she blinked them away. She had no right to cry.

Tom said, "We've reason to believe the game originated while Sophie was still living at home."

Jackson's eyes flashed angrily. "Just what the hell are you implying?"

His outburst seemed to surprise Tom even though she'd warned him about Jackson's disposition. "I'm not implying anything. I'm trying to establish whether anyone new had come into Sophie's life before she went to stay with Rae. The fourth player remains a mystery. We'd like to find out who that person is."

Rae thought about Sophie's time with her. "Hannah Tucker and Dylan Moody were the only two who ever came to my house. You saw them there this morning. If Sophie hung out with anyone else, I never saw them."

Jackson pounced. "Have you questioned the Moody kid yet? I wouldn't put anything past that punk. Look at how he was brought up. His old man's never been anything but trouble. I've known Dwight Moody since high school. You try to cut him a break, he's apt to turn around and stab you in the back. But if there's one thing he's good at, it's sniffing out easy money. I wouldn't be surprised if he and the kid are in this together."

Tom said slowly, "Are you saying you think Sophie was taken for money?"

Too late Jackson realized his mistake. He opened his mouth and then shut it again as he searched for a way out.

Whether her intent or not, Lauren came to his rescue. She gave him a contemptuous stare. "You're jumping to conclusions because you don't like Dylan. That boy didn't take Sophie. He'd never do anything to hurt her."

Jackson spun to face his wife, transferring his frustration onto her. "And you know this how?"

"I've seen them together. He's crazy about her." Defiance sparked as Lauren lifted her chin and glared at her husband. Something was definitely going on between them. An undercurrent of hostility that couldn't be feigned. The pair had never been shy about arguing in public. They both had quick tempers and acerbic tongues, but the rancor simmering between them now was something new. Something dark and disturbing.

Lauren's taunt pushed all the wrong buttons, as she had undoubtedly meant for it to. Jackson took a step toward her. "Why are you defending that little creep? If I didn't know better, I'd almost think—"

"What?" Lauren rose slowly to confront him. "What would you think?"

He stared her down for a moment without speaking. Then he jabbed a finger in the air in Rae's direction without looking at her. "You're as much to blame for this as she is. If it wasn't for you, Sophie would still be home, where she belongs."

Lauren's eyes flared knowingly. "I'm not the reason Sophie left home. She couldn't wait to get away from *you*."

The nasty argument dissolved into another stare down. Rae sat watching them in dread and fascination. Why were they doing this in front of Tom Brannon, of all people? Didn't they know he would be taking all of this in? Rae's gaze darted to the sheriff. One thing was certain. The confrontation had taken the focus off Jackson's gaffe. Without another word, her brother whirled and started toward the door.

"Where do you think you're going?" Lauren called after him.

"To find that stupid kid. I'll beat the truth out of him if I have to."

Rae jumped to her feet and grabbed her brother's arm. "Just calm down—"

He shoved her aside. She stumbled and fell back against the chair. Tom was in Jackson's face in a flash. "Touch her again and I'll put you in cuffs."

"Get out of my way or I'll have your badge."

Tom didn't budge. "You can try, but it won't stop me from doing my job. You start trouble with that boy and I'll have no choice but to take you in."

"He's right," Rae said. "Just back off and let the man do his job."

"Do his *job*? You mean the same way his old man found our sister?"

The phone rang just then and Jackson's sneer vanished. Rae could see her brother's profile. In that moment, his rage deflated and he looked as terrified as she felt. Her gaze flashed to her father's desk. Everyone in the room seemed to freeze, including West Cavanaugh. Then he lifted the handset to his ear. After a gruff hello, he listened for a moment and then said, "I can't talk now. You'll have to call back later." He slammed the phone down and stood.

"Dad?" Rae half rose, too.

He put up a hand to stop her. "I'm going outside for some air. Don't anyone try to follow me. I've had my fill of the lot of you." His gaze pierced Jackson. "Get yourself together. If you have to air your dirty laundry in this house, do it behind closed doors. And you." He turned to Rae. "You brought the sheriff in here, you can damn well show him to the door."

## *Chapter Seven*

West stepped out into the garden and slammed the door behind him. Rae wanted to follow. She wanted to know if one of the kidnappers had been on the other end of that call, but she couldn't say anything with Tom still present. Jackson wavered as if debating on whether or not to defy their dad's wishes. Then he turned and stormed out of the room. Lauren followed him out into the hallway, where they continued to bicker until their voices faded behind another slammed door.

Tom turned to Rae. "That went well."

She gave a shaky laugh to relieve tension. "Didn't it? As well as could be expected, knowing my family the way I do. Come on. I'll walk you to your car."

All the way down the hallway, she was conscious of Tom's sidelong gaze. He had to be curious about the scene that had just gone down between Jackson and his wife, about the phone call, Rae's behavior and everything else. He said nothing, but his silence spoke volumes.

Once they were outside, she surreptitiously glanced in the back seat of her car on the way to his vehicle. The bag was still there, thank goodness.

She leaned against his door and turned her face to the sky. A hawk circled overhead. She watched for a moment, but the sky was so brilliant she had to look away. Exhaustion tugged. With very little effort, she could drift off. Just close her eyes and float away from this whole awful mess. How could a day be so beautiful on the surface and so ugly underneath?

"Rae?"

She opened her eyes.

"Are you okay? You're very quiet all of a sudden."

"Just lost in thought. I can only imagine what you must think of us after that embarrassing display."

"I think you're a family in crisis," he said. "You've lost a mother, a sister, and now you're afraid you may be facing another tragedy."

His compassion brought tears to her eyes. She took a moment to gather her composure. "It's true what they say about the waiting. The not knowing. It wears on you. All the terrible things that go through your head. Your mind never shuts down. You can't sleep. You can't eat. You start to dread the sound of the phone. Then comes the time when the phone stops ringing and the silence is even more terrifying."

Tom gave her one of those soft gazes, the kind that tore at her resolve. She thought again how nice it would be to feel those strong arms around her, to have his broad shoulder to lean on. She wasn't a needy person. She'd always been fiercely independent and proud of it. But this wasn't about need. It was about comfort and understanding. The solace of having someone next to you who'd have your back no matter what. Rae loved her father and brother, but she couldn't honestly say that she trusted them to always have her best interest at heart. They were too arrogant and single-minded.

"I know it's hard," Tom said. "But Sophie isn't Riley. She didn't disappear without a trace. She left a trail."

Rae tucked back her hair. "You mean the text messages?"

"Among other things. We won't rest until we follow every bread crumb." He glanced over his shoulder at the house. "Your brother worries me, though. I meant what I said inside. If he goes after the Moody boy, I'll have no choice but to lock him up."

"He won't," Rae said. "He was just letting off steam."

"Does he always get physical when he lets off steam?"

She frowned. "You mean what happened just now? That was nothing. A sibling skirmish. Besides, I'm the one who started it. I grabbed his arm, he pushed me away and I tripped. Please don't make more of it than it was. Don't you and your sister ever fight?"

"We have the occasional disagreement."

"Occasional." Her smiled turned bitter. "Most families aren't perfect."

Tom's gaze was still on her. She didn't want to look up into those rain-colored eyes, but she couldn't help herself. He moved in, not so close as to be threatening, but enough so that the space between them grew intimate. She could almost imagine his hand on her arm, his knuckles scraping softly against her cheek. *Everything will be all right, Rae.*

Instead, he said, "I'm not your enemy. You need to trust me."

She let out a slow breath, releasing the anger she'd been harboring for hours. Not at Tom this time, but at her brother. At her niece's abductors. At her feeling of helplessness. "I'm trying to. I want to trust you. It's just…"

"My sister came home and yours didn't."

"Yes." She folded her arms. "As irrational and petty as that still sounds."

"Then I don't know what more I can say. Do you honestly think my dad didn't do everything in his power to find Riley? Do you think he wouldn't have given his own life to bring her home safely? Do you think I wouldn't? Not a day goes by that I don't think about what happened. I've asked myself a thousand times what I might have done differently to change the outcome. If I'd gotten to the Ruins sooner or if I hadn't let down my guard. If I'd never left the house that night in the first place." He paused, but his gaze never wavered. "I don't know why my sister and I were spared. I don't think it was intentional. I've always believed we were left for dead. What I do know is that Ellie wasn't breathing when I came to. I had to act fast. Make a split-second decision. I could have left her there on the bank to go back and search the Ruins, but letting my sister die wouldn't have saved yours. Deep down, I think you know that."

His blunt assessment took Rae's breath away. Her brother wasn't the only one who could wound her with words. "We all do what we have to do," she murmured.

She wondered if he would be so understanding of her decision to keep quiet when he found out about the ransom demand. If the kidnappers let Sophie go, all would be forgiven eventually. But if her niece never came home, Rae would spend the rest of her life playing the same terrible game of what-if. What if she'd told Tom the truth? What if she'd gone to him with the ransom demand and asked for his help?

His gaze narrowed. "What did you mean by that?"

"Just what I said. Most of us do what we think is right in any given situation. Second-guessing is pointless. I just wish there was something more I could do right now. Some way I could help with the investigation."

He was still eyeing her with what Rae thought might be suspicion. "What can you tell me about Blaine Fenton?"

The name took Rae by surprise. "Blaine? Why do you want to know about him?"

"His family owns an adjoining ranch. I understand his father is suing Cavanaugh Industries. There must be bad blood between the families."

Rae shrugged. "I can't tell you much about that lawsuit. I'm not involved."

He looked skeptical. "You're the money person in the business. How can you not be involved?"

"My brother calls the shots now. He and my father have deliberately kept me out of the loop. I like to think they're trying to protect me, but I suspect the attorneys have advised them I could have a conflict of interest."

"What kind of conflict?"

"Blaine and I were once engaged."

The gray eyes flickered though his voice remained steady. "When was this?"

"About a hundred years ago," Rae said with a grimace. "We dated before he went into the service. When he came home, we tried to pick back up where we left off, but it was too late. I wore his ring on my finger for all of a week before I realized I wasn't ready for that kind of commitment."

"You broke things off? How did he take it?"

Rae sensed a sudden tension. She said carefully, "About as well as you can imagine."

"Did he get violent? Make threats? Anything like that?"

"No. He left town without a word. We didn't keep in touch. I heard that he came back when his dad got sick, but I haven't seen or talked to him." She slanted Tom a puzzled glance. "Why all these questions about Blaine? You don't think he had anything to do with Sophie's disappearance, do you?"

"He's convinced your family swindled his sick father out of a lot of money. That's a powerful motive. So is rejection."

"You think he's carrying a grudge against *me*?" The notion that Sophie had been taken because of Rae's past was another painful blow. "If that's true, why didn't he come after me personally? Why take Sophie?"

"She was living with you when she went missing. He'd know how her disappearance would affect you."

She was silent for a moment. "I don't believe it. It's been too many years. Besides, Blaine wouldn't do something like that. He's always been a good guy."

"You said you hadn't had any contact with him in years. People change. Or sometimes something happens to bring out their true nature."

"That's a scary thought."

"People do scary things," Tom said. "Is there anyone else you can think of who might have it in for you or your family?"

"We've been in business for a long time. My dad and brother aren't the easiest people to deal with. We've had our share of bitter competitors and disgruntled former employees, but I'm not aware of any physical threats. As for me personally, my opinion pieces for the *Star* have ruffled a few feathers. I don't tend to pull punches."

"I'm well aware of that fact."

"Tom." She suppressed a shiver. "Do you really think Sophie could have been taken because of me?"

"Whatever the abductor's motive, this isn't your fault."

He stared deep into her eyes as something shifted between them. Any rancor that might have remained melted in the face of his compassion. Before Rae could stop herself, she placed her hand on his arm, unconsciously reaching for his warmth. "Find her, Tom. I can only imagine how frightened she must be. Please bring her home."

"I'll do everything in my power. You know that."

She nodded and dropped her hand as her gaze traveled down the long drive, probing into the woods and then returning to skim the shadowy windows. Physical contact was inadvisable. Someone could be watching. From outside the house and from within.

RAE DIDN'T LEAVE the ranch again until late that night. After Tom drove away, she'd taken the money inside and locked it away in the safe. The housekeeper had made sandwiches and iced tea for a late lunch, but no one was hungry. The casserole she made for dinner went virtually untouched, as well. They sat huddled in her father's office until the sun set over her mother's rose garden and the bats came out of their houses. Rae stood at the French doors and watched them circle until they vanished against the deepening sky. One by one the stars twinkled out and the moon rose over the treetops. And still no word of Sophie. Still no phone call from the kidnappers.

They were all scared and bone-deep weary. Rae wanted a shower and her own bed, but she was reluctant to leave her father alone on the ranch with all that cash. Not that he would be truly alone. The housekeeper had quarters off the kitchen and the ranch foreman lived on the property. The house was well secured and her father well armed, but if he was right and they were dealing with professional kidnappers, anything could happen.

"Go home," Jackson finally insisted. "You're dead on your feet and no help to anyone. I'll stay with Dad. I want to be here in case we get another call. Just let me run home and change clothes before you leave. Lauren can stay at our house in case anyone decides to call the landline there."

Lauren nodded her acquiescence and the two of them left. They were barely speaking by this time. Maybe it was a good thing they had another night apart.

Jackson returned a little while later and Rae hugged her father good-night. All the way home, she kept an eye on the rearview mirror. Once, a car came upon her so quickly she became certain someone was trying to overtake her to force her off the road. She gripped the wheel as the car passed and sped off into the night. By the time she drove into town, her neck and shoulders ached from tension.

Fueled by the strain and a pervasive dread, her imagination went to bad places. She'd never noticed before how dark the streets were in her neighborhood. The old-fashioned streetlamps were quaint but not effective in holding the night at bay. Everywhere she looked, she saw lurking shadows.

Pulling into the garage, she lowered the door all the way before getting out of her car. Once inside the house, she turned the dead bolt. She rarely bothered with the security system, but she felt the need to activate the sensors tonight. After checking to make sure the garden doors were secured, she went straight upstairs to the shower and stood under the hot water until phantom sounds drove her dripping from the bathroom. Wrapping herself in a towel, she padded across her bedroom into the hallway, then to the staircase, where she glanced down into the foyer.

*No one's there. You're safe.* Sophie was the one in danger.

But even as Rae shrugged off the night sounds, uneasiness dogged her back to the bathroom. She couldn't shake the sensation that someone had been inside her house while she was away. Finishing her bedtime routine, she opened the door to the hallway before crawling between the cool sheets. If a sound came from anywhere in the house, she would hear it.

She didn't think she'd be able to sleep a wink, but she grew drowsy the moment her head hit the pillow. She'd just dozed off when one of those sounds catapulted her upright in bed.

No one could get into the house through a door or window without tripping the sensors and setting off the alarm. But what if someone had already been inside when she got home?

Throwing off the covers, she swung her legs over the side of the bed and perched on the edge as she listened to the house. She'd almost convinced herself she'd dreamed the noise when she heard it again, so low and distant she couldn't pinpoint the source or location. She padded to the hallway door and glanced out. She'd left a light burning at the top of the stairs. Keeping her back to the wall, she eased once again to the landing and glanced into the foyer. She started down the stairs when the noise froze her again. She recognized the muffled reverberation this time. It was the sound of a phone that had been set to both ring and vibrate.

Returning to her bedroom, she grabbed her cell from the nightstand charger and checked her screen even though she knew the strange ringtone wasn't hers. Then whose?

Was someone in the house with her at that very moment?

She pocketed the cell and returned to the hallway, tracking the sound past the guest bathroom and bedroom to Sophie's room. Pushing open the door, she hovered on the threshold as she gazed around. Moonlight and a night breeze flooded in through the open window. Her pulse leaped as the curtains billowed. For a moment, she was certain someone stood behind them. Then the wind died away and the gauzy panels flattened. Only then did she remember closing the window the night before. It had been shut that morning when she stood looking down into the rose garden as Tom searched the room behind her.

The ringing had stopped by this time. Rae checked the bathroom and closet and then dropped to the floor to search under the bed. Rising, she crossed the room to the window and peered down into the garden. Was someone down there watching her? A shadow moved and she jumped. A dog barked and she jumped.

Hand to her heart, she turned to scan the room once more. Her gaze fell on the bed and she traced a faint impression in the chenille spread as if someone had been lying there recently. The idea was so frightening and repugnant, Rae wanted to run screaming from the house, but the sudden *vzzzzt* of that vibrating ringtone froze her.

As if in a dream, she walked to the bed and picked up one of the pillows. Sophie's image stared up at her from a cell phone screen. She was bound and gagged, her face bruised and tear-streaked. But she was alive. Or had been when the photo was taken.

Reluctantly, Rae accepted the incoming call. "Hello?"

A metallic voice said in her ear, "Call the police and she dies. Call the FBI and she dies. Come alone to the drop or you die."

# *Chapter Eight*

The next morning, Tom stood at the back of the
conference room while Craig Jarvis updated the
department's active investigations on the white-
board and handed out assignments to the as-
sembled officers. He tried to concentrate on the
business at hand, but his mind kept straying to the
previous day's events, in particular to the scene
he'd witnessed at the ranch. The bitterness between Jackson and Lauren Cavanaugh had been
palpable. He'd been shocked by the nastiness
of Jackson's attack and the underlying vicious-
ness of Lauren's volley. If they fought like that
on a regular basis, no wonder their daughter had
wanted to run away.

He thought about Rae, too, and her revelation
that she'd once been engaged to Blaine Fenton.
Tom didn't know how he felt about that. The relationship was ancient history and likely had
nothing to do with Sophie's disappearance. On
the other hand, the bad blood between Fenton

and the Cavanaughs provided a motive and Tom wasn't about to leave any stone unturned. A cursory background check had turned up an interesting detail and Tom thought it might be time to pay Fenton a visit.

After the officers had filed out of the room, he and Craig conferred for a few minutes and then went their separate ways. Back in his office, Tom scoured a county map, familiarizing himself with the terrain surrounding the Fenton ranch. Then he plugged the address into his GPS and headed out. The excursion took him deep into the swampy bottomland of Nance County. As the road narrowed, the pine forest grew denser until only streamers of sunlight filtered down through the bowers. The air was steamy and pungent, the shadows so deep on either side of the road that Tom could understand how the primitive landscape spawned tall tales of swamp creatures and black panthers.

A metal cattle guard across a paved lane marked the entrance to the ranch. The one-story brick house was modest in comparison with the Cavanaugh spread, but the trim looked freshly painted and the roof appeared new. Despite the hardships the family had suffered, someone had recently infused money into the property.

Tom got out of his vehicle and took stock of his surroundings before climbing the porch steps to knock on the door. When no one answered, he followed a footpath back to the barn. One of the double doors hung open and he thought Blaine Fenton might be working inside.

Calling out the man's name, he stepped from bright sunlight into the dim, cavernous interior. A barrage of scents greeted him—leather, hay and diesel mixed with the lingering aroma of horses. The animals were long gone, replaced with a small fleet of four-wheelers. Tom walked down the row of empty stalls, checked the tack room and was on his way back to the front when a furtive sound halted him. His gaze lifted as a few bits of hay floated down through the cracks in the loft.

He went up the steps as quietly as he could, pausing at the top to reconnoiter. The space looked like any other barn loft he'd encountered with a wide-plank floor and overhead rafters. Some of the bales of hay had been broken apart and piled on the floor, creating a cozy mattress where someone had recently slept. An old blanket had been neatly folded and stored on a bench, along with a towel and a bucket of basic toiletries.

The only occupant up there now was a fat yellow tabby that crouched at the top of the haystack, eyeing the intruder with sleepy-eyed suspicion. Tom had a quick look around before the hum of a four-wheeler drove him back down the steps.

By the time he got to the front of the barn, the motor had died. A moment later, Blaine Fenton appeared in the doorway with a shotgun.

Tom approached with caution, moving his hand to his side where he could draw his weapon if he needed to.

"It's Tom Brannon," he called out.

Fenton hesitated and then took a step inside, dropping the barrel of the shotgun toward the floor. "Sheriff? What the hell are you doing in here?"

His tone wasn't as cordial or deferential as he'd seemed in Tom's office. Fair enough. He'd been caught by surprise. Tom tried to defuse the situation. "I need to have a word. I knocked at the house first, but no one answered. When I saw the barn door was open, I thought you might be back here working." His gaze flicked to the shotgun. "Mind putting that away while we talk?"

Fenton propped the weapon against the wall. "Sorry about that. I'm in the habit of arming myself before I go out. I don't even think about having it with me anymore."

"You expecting trouble?"

"In this part of the county? Damn right. We're remote and lousy with meth heads. They'll steal anything that isn't nailed down. And they tend to get violent when confronted. I guess I don't have to tell you that."

"Pays to be careful," Tom agreed. "But if you're that worried about thieves, I'd suggest locking up before you leave. Unless you're expecting someone." He chin-nodded toward the loft. "Looks like someone's being staying up there. One of your ranch hands?"

"Pop has a few regulars that come by now and then. He gives them a hot meal and a place to clean up and sleep."

"What do you mean by regulars?"

"Not PC to call them hoboes anymore. Guys that ride the rails. They get on and off at the crossing by the river. Pop's been letting them stay here for years. Harmless for the most part, but I've warned him about keeping the doors up at the house locked."

*For the most part.* He had Tom's attention. "When was the last time someone came by?"

"I'd say a couple of weeks at least." Fenton appeared more relaxed now. Leaning a shoulder against the wall, he slid his hands in his pockets. "What did you want to talk to me about? I said everything I had to say when I came by the station."

Tom studied the man's expression, his posture. Fenton had reverted back to his polite comportment, but there was a troubling vibe in that barn. "Why didn't you tell me that you and Rae Cavanaugh were once engaged?"

Fenton shrugged but the tension seemed to amp up a notch. "That was a long time ago. What happened between Rae and me has nothing to do with anything."

"I don't know about that," Tom said. "It gives you a motive."

And just like that, the polite veneer vanished, allowing a simmering bitterness to cast a shadow over the man's features. He flexed his fingers as if to remind Tom that the shotgun was still within easy reach. "A motive for what? Maybe you'd better get to the point of this visit, Sheriff."

"You made some pretty bold accusations about Rae and her family. A broken engagement could explain why you were so keen to paint her in an unflattering light."

"I take it she's the one who told you about our split?"

Tom didn't comment.

"I don't know how she presented things to you, but there's always another side to the story. I won't bother telling you mine. What's past is past." Fenton shrugged again, as if trying to free himself of an unwanted ghost. "Rae Cavanaugh could be an angel these days, for all I care. I came to you because I wanted you to know about the lawsuit. About *their* motives. If I'd known you'd try to turn it all back on me, I would have kept my mouth shut."

Tom waited a beat before he said, "You also didn't tell me about your record. Assault with a deadly weapon is serious business."

He could see the man working to control his temper. "So you pulled my sheet. Before or after you talked to Rae?"

"Does it matter?"

"If you've done your homework, then you know the original charge was downgraded to a misdemeanor. I did nine months in a county lockup, but the arrest was bogus from the get-go. Guy came at me with a knife and I defended myself with a broken bottle. We both ended up in the ER, but he had connections and I didn't. You know how that goes. The sentencing judge was removed from the bench and did time himself for accepting bribes. I was clean before that night and I've been clean ever since. Nothing in my past has a damn thing to do with why I came to your office."

"Where were you on Thursday night?"

Fenton's gaze narrowed. "On the night of the kidnapping, you mean."

"It's a routine question," Tom said.

He could have sworn the man's gaze strayed to the shotgun before he answered. "I was in Dallas. Pop is in the hospital again. I stayed with him for most of the day, took care of some business, and then I had a bite to eat with a friend. I got back to the ranch around midnight."

"Can anyone corroborate your arrival time?"

"Like I said, Pop's in the hospital, so there's no one here but me. You can talk to him, I guess. I can give you my friend's number if you insist, but I'd rather not get her involved."

"I may need her name," Tom said. "But that's all for now. I'll be in touch."

Fenton walked him outside. "Have you talked to the Cavanaughs? Did you question them about *their* whereabouts?"

"I've talked to a lot of people, but I can't get into any of the details of those conversations."

Fenton's tone turned grim. "I hope you find that girl soon, Sheriff. If the family didn't set this up, she could be in real trouble. I keep thinking about Riley."

"We're all thinking about Riley," Tom said as he glanced around the property. He made sure Fenton remained in his periphery as he took note of the other outbuildings. "You're right about one thing. You are isolated out here. Keep a sharp eye as you go about your business. You see or hear anything suspicious, give me a call."

Fenton put up a hand to shade his eyes as he, too, scoured the countryside. "Lots of abandoned houses and barns in these parts. People use them for all sorts of unsavory activities. I try not to snoop in the wrong places. I don't want to get my head blown off. But I will keep an eye out. And next time you want to talk, maybe you should call first. Like I said, I arm myself before I leave the house. You can't be too careful these days."

Tom nodded. "I'll keep that in mind."

Fenton closed and latched the barn doors before trailing Tom back to the house. He climbed the porch steps, but he didn't go inside. Instead, he stood leaning against the railing as he watched Tom get into his vehicle. Tom gave a brief nod, but Fenton didn't bother responding. He'd left his shotgun in the barn, but Tom had no doubt the man had more than one weapon at his disposal.

After a decade in law enforcement, Tom appreciated the need for caution and self-defense. Drugs and human trafficking had created a dangerous situation in rural areas all over the state. Nance County was no exception. Gone were the days when people routinely left doors and windows open at all hours or when kids could roam the countryside without fear of being accosted or nabbed. Tom thought about his sister out there alone on the lake. Her place was secure, and she knew how to use a gun, but Tom still worried about her. Sometimes he thought they might both be living on borrowed time.

He glanced in his rearview mirror as he drove away from the house. Blaine Fenton was still on the porch staring after him. Tom wasn't sure how he felt about their discussion. On the one hand, Fenton had been forthcoming about the nature of his incarceration; on the other, he'd kept that information to himself until confronted. Tom had to wonder what else he might be hiding.

He slowed as he neared the cattle guard. Before he could cross, another car whipped off the road and braked. Tom recognized Rae's SUV. Rather than reversing to let her pass, he put the vehicle in Park and got out. Rae got out, too, and they met on her side of the grid.

She looked shocked to see him and, unless Tom misread her averted gaze, a little guilty. Unease niggled as she approached him. "Tom? What are you doing out here?"

The sun beat down on his shoulders as he gave her a long scrutiny. He could see freckles beneath her suntan and the dark purple half-moons of fatigue and distress beneath her eyes. "I think it's best if you answer that question first."

She hesitated. "I guess you could call it an impulse."

"What kind of impulse?" The question came out harsher than Tom meant, but Rae didn't seem to notice. Her gaze drifted to the narrow road behind him. Even though they were out of sight of the house, he imagined Blaine Fenton up on that porch staring back at her.

A shadow passed across her features as if she'd had the same thought. "I keep going over our conversation yesterday and your implication that Blaine might still hold a grudge against me. I don't think it's true. The breakup was a long time ago. But on the slim chance you could be right, I wanted to see his face when I asked him flat out if he had anything to do with Sophie's disappearance."

"You drove all the way out here to confront him? That's not a good idea, Rae."

"Why not?" A frown flitted as her gaze turned defiant. "I'll be able to tell if he's lying."

"You sure about that?"

"It's worth a shot, isn't it?" She wore her hair down today and the mild breeze that stirred the long brown tresses seemed to annoy her. She tucked the errant strands behind her ears with a jerky movement.

Tom tried to keep his voice neutral without seeming to patronize her. "Just think it through for a minute. Aside from the fact that you haven't seen Fenton in years, what if he really did have something to do with Sophie's disappearance? What do you think will happen if he feels threatened? He'll tie up loose ends and make a run for it."

She looked stricken. "Tie up loose ends? What do you mean?"

"Leave no witnesses behind." Tom hated being so blunt. "We can't take that chance."

"Then why are you here? He's bound to feel more heat from you than me. What makes you think he won't panic and run after you talked to him?"

"Because I'm the law. I'm asking a lot of questions of a lot of people. He'll know that if he has his ear to the ground. Given his history with your family, it would seem strange if I didn't talk to him." Tom tempered his tone as he gazed down at her, resisting the almost physical need to touch her. What was it about Rae Cavanaugh that had him wound up so tight? Why couldn't he just do his damn job and keep emotions out of it? "You have to trust that I know what I'm doing. Just go home and let me handle this."

"I can't go home, Tom. I can't stand the waiting." She turned to gaze off into the trees. "I was out all morning searching the woods around the Ruins and walking up and down the lake. I saw your sister. She said officers have been out there since sunrise. I know that's your doing. Thank you for that. Thank you for not giving up."

"It's way too early to talk about giving up."

She nodded. "I wanted to go inside the Ruins, but the doors are cordoned off."

"That's standard procedure," he said. "Not that tape is much of a barrier in a place like that. People are curious about such things. We don't have enough manpower to keep them out."

"Then it's okay if I go inside?"

"Why would you want to? We've been all through that building, including the basement and boiler room. If anything besides Sophie's phone had been left behind, we would have found it by now."

"You mentioned symbols yesterday. I want to see them for myself."

"Why?"

She seemed at a loss. "I don't know why. Maybe I'm curious about such things, too. Maybe I'm wondering why Sophie would willingly play a game that trivialized Riley's disappearance."

She looked so distraught standing there gazing up at him. So earnest and desperate, and Tom felt dangerously protective even though Rae Cavanaugh could take care of herself. She was worried, yes. Scared, yes. But there was a dauntless quality to the way she held herself, a steely resolve to the set of her jaw and chin when she didn't want to be told no. Her intrepid nature made him want to protect her all the more, which made no sense. His feelings for Rae Cavanaugh made no sense. He'd known her for most of his life. Had admired her good looks from afar since they were kids, but never once had he thought about her in *that* way. She'd been off-limits. A prickly nemesis who had kept him and most every other man in Nance County at arm's length. But not Blaine Fenton.

A vision crept around Tom's subconscious, unnerving him in the morning heat. He wasn't jealous. That would really be pushing boundaries. But he didn't like thinking about Rae and Blaine Fenton as a couple. He didn't like imagining them together or wondering if she'd told him the real reason she'd shown up at the Fenton ranch so early in the morning.

He especially didn't like all those gnawing doubts.

She looked distressed as her gaze moved back to the road behind him. "Do you think he can see us from the house?"

"No. Those trees block the view." Tom glanced over his shoulder anyway. They couldn't be spotted from the house, but her question prodded him. "Let's get moving. We're standing on Fenton property and your ex-fiancé could head this way at any minute with his shotgun. I'd rather not find out how willing he is to use it."

"Tom?" Her eyes held him enthralled. "I was never in love with Blaine Fenton. I'm not sure why, but I want you to know that."

TOM FOLLOWED HER as far as the arched entrance to the Cavanaugh ranch, and then with a honk and a wave, he headed back toward town. Rae drove only a short way before she pulled to the side of the road and cut the engine. Her hands shook. She lifted them from the wheel and observed the tremor in her fingers. Tom Brannon had done that to her. Unsettled her. Intimidated her. Made her want to wrap her arms around his neck and kiss him until all her dark thoughts fled.

Lowering the window, Rae drew in the pungent air. She'd parked in deep shade, and the breeze blowing through the pine forest felt cool against her overheated face. She told herself to buck up. She couldn't let the family see her so rattled. They needed her. She'd always been the steady one, a rock in times of crises, but at that moment, she'd never felt less in control. Sophie's disappearance had leveled all her defenses, and her unwelcome attraction to Tom Brannon had only intensified an already desperate situation.

She chided herself for the weakness. How could she feel anything at that moment except frightened? The kidnapping had her all knotted up inside and yet somehow Tom Brannon had managed to pierce through her fear. Maybe it really was as simple as needing a friend, a strong shoulder, and if anyone could understand her angst, it was Tom.

Still, she had to be careful. He was a lawman trained to look for nuances and tells. The more time she spent in his company, the greater the chance she'd let something slip. She hated keeping secrets, especially with Sophie's life on the line, but the kidnappers had left her no choice. *Call the police and she dies.*

After receiving that message loud and clear the night before, Rae had raced back to the ranch, calling on the way so that her father and brother wouldn't be alarmed when she turned up at the door. They'd huddled around the kitchen table, downing shots of whiskey as they discussed the next step. Jackson had wanted to take charge of the kidnappers' phone, but Rae refused. The burner had been left in her house. The threat had been made directly to her. For whatever reason, she'd been designated the point person.

Keeping that phone close, Rae had gone out at the crack of dawn to search for Sophie. Maybe that was the wrong thing to do. Rationally, she knew the best way to help her niece was to sit tight. They had the money and they had proof of life. The rest was a waiting game. But Rae had never been strong on patience. The futile search had been more for her benefit than Sophie's. She couldn't sit around drowning in despair. Taking action, no matter how pointless, kept her focused and grounded, which was why she'd gone out to the Fenton ranch.

She didn't really believe Blaine could be involved, but what if he was? She needed to see

his face, stare deeply into his eyes to know if
there was anything left of the old Blaine. Even as
kids, she'd always been able to tell when he lied.
He'd been an open book. Or so she'd thought.
But how well had she ever really known him?
They'd drifted together because of the proximity of their family ranches and a common up-
bringing. He used to say that East Texans were
a different breed, a mixture of Southern gen-
tility and backwoods cliquishness, so they had
to stick together. He was one of the few people who understood her, one of the few people
who had never tried to change her. Undemand-
ing and uncomplicated, Blaine Fenton had been
an easy man to like, and for a time, Rae had tried
to convince herself that she could love him. That
hadn't worked out. Maybe she wasn't the marry-
ing kind. Or maybe she'd sensed something even
then, hunkering down deep inside him.

Taking out the burner, Rae studied the photograph of Sophie. She looked so young and helpless and scared. Tenderly, Rae traced the girl's
battered features with her fingertip. The gag was
hard enough to witness, but the scratches and
bruises that marred the smooth cheeks tore at
Rae's heart.

*She's alive. That's all that matters. Just do as the
kidnappers instruct and this will all be over soon.*

Rae desperately wanted to believe in a positive

outcome. Sophie wasn't Riley. This could still work out if they all kept their cool—

A cloud of blackbirds lifted from the woods in a flurry of flapping wings. Rae's head snapped up as she scoured the countryside. Something had startled them from the treetops, but everything else had gone silent. On any given day, at any given time, the forest teemed with life, but the rabbits and squirrels had scurried to the safety of their hidey-holes.

Into that deathly hush came the sound of the kidnappers' ringtone. The burner phone vibrated in Rae's hand. Several clicks went by before she pressed the accept call button. She put the phone on speaker and the grating sound of that mechanical voice filled her vehicle.

"You talked to the cops."

She suppressed a gasp at the accusation. "No, I didn't. I didn't talk to anyone."

"You talked to the cops."

"I didn't! I saw Sheriff Brannon this morning, but I didn't say a word and I won't." She gulped back her panic. "He's investigating Sophie's disappearance. He has questions. If we don't appear to cooperate, he'll get suspicious—"

The call dropped.

A moment later, the phone dinged an incoming text. Rae clicked the message icon and a video appeared. Her thumb hovered over the arrow before she pressed Play. Sophie came into view. She was tied to a chair with a high window behind her, but not much light filtered in. Either the video had been shot in the dark or the grounds outside were in deep shadow.

Rae tried to take note of the surroundings, but her gaze remained riveted on her niece. She looked terrified but determined as she struggled and strained against the bindings. Then she went suddenly still. Her head pivoted as if someone had entered the room. The sound of a gunshot startled Rae so badly she screamed, and then the video ended.

Numb with shock, she stared at the screen in helpless fear. Then she shook the phone as if she could somehow bring Sophie back.

"No. Please, no…" *Please, please, please, please…*

A split second of mindless panic crawled by before Rae realized the gunfire had come from the woods and not the video. Another flock of birds had taken to the sky in alarm. Someone was out there.

Leaning forward to peer out the windshield, she reached for the ignition and then her hand froze. Was Sophie nearby? The gunshot had been a warning, but if the weapon had been fired from the location where Sophie was being held—

Rae was out of her vehicle in a flash, standing

in the middle of the road with her ears trained on the woods. Conjuring a map, she tried to recall any nearby buildings, old barns and farmhouses where the kidnappers might hold Sophie. *Where are you?*

Jumping the ditch, she moved to the edge of the trees. "I know you're out there!" she yelled. "I know you can hear me! We have the money! All we want is Sophie! Please, please don't hurt her!"

No sound came to Rae, nothing so much as the snapping of a twig, but she could sense a presence. *Who are you?*

"Just tell me where to leave the money. We can end this today. No one has to get hurt."

Her voice echoed back to her as she stood there searching the trees. She thought about Tom's theory that the game had been used to lure Sophie to the Ruins alone, which meant at least one of the kidnappers knew her. A friend or an acquaintance. Someone familiar with Riley's abduction and Sophie's fascination with the past.

For one terrible moment, rage clouded Rae's vision, a white-hot fury that someone could be so cruel as to terrorize a child in order to extort money from an already devastated family. Rae's impulse now was to tear through the woods until she found the offenders. She wanted nothing so much at that moment as to feel her hands around a throat. To hear that voice on the phone plead with *her*.

Tamping down such a reckless inclination, she called out again. "Tell me where to leave the money! *Please*. We just want her home."

The blackbirds circled as a chill invaded. She could stand there all day begging and bargaining, but the kidnappers wouldn't make contact again until they were ready. They knew what they were doing, how to instill fear and cooperation. Sophie's abduction had taken long-term planning and skill. A trap had been patiently laid. Nothing had been left to chance. And no loose end would be left untied when it was over.

"Please," Rae whispered. "Just take the money."

She jumped when the phone vibrated in her hand. Accepting the call, she scanned the woods. Off to her right, a shadow moved, or was that her imagination?

The robotic voice said into the quiet, "Be smart. We're watching you."

# Chapter Nine

Later that morning, Dylan Moody and Hannah Tucker appeared at the station at the agreed-upon time. One of Tom's detectives had already conducted an informal interview with both kids, but Tom wanted to get them on the record. Plus, it was easier to evade and outright lie in the safety of their homes than it was in an institutional environment. They had no idea what the police already knew or who might be observing—and contradicting—their statements through a two-way glass.

Unlike Hannah, who waited in another area of the station with her mother, Dylan had come in alone. He said his old man had been too busy to accompany him. Too hungover, more than likely. Jackson Cavanaugh wasn't the only one who'd had unpleasant dealings with Dwight Moody. Back when Tom was still on patrol, he'd been sent out to the Moody place on any number of 10-16s—domestic disturbances—before Dwight's girlfriend had finally left him for good. Dylan hadn't been so lucky.

He sat with his shoulders hunched and his eyes downcast, his posture and demeanor a far cry from the punk whom Jackson Cavanaugh had described the day before. Craig Jarvis conducted the interview while Tom observed from a dimmed area on the other side of the glass. Dylan's answers had been mostly monosyllabic at first, but once Craig mentioned the group text messages, the kid's head came up and the floodgates opened. To Tom's surprise, Dylan readily copped to his participation in the game.

"I don't understand," Craig said. "You saw Sheriff Brannon at Rae Cavanaugh's house yesterday morning. Why didn't you tell him about the game then? You made it sound as if you never went out to the Ruins."

Dylan pushed back a lock of dark hair from his forehead. He seemed willing to talk, but he was nervous as hell about something. "Sophie made us promise not to tell anyone. She said her stepmother already wanted to get rid of her. If she found out that Sophie was sneaking out of the house at night, she'd make sure her dad sent her away to boarding school."

"You didn't think her safety trumped that promise?"

Dylan winced. "I didn't think she was in any

danger. Not at first." His legs were jittery beneath the table. He wiped his hands along the tops of his thighs. "I thought she was just hiding out. Or maybe she ran away. She's done it before. I kept thinking she'd call or text, but she hasn't. Now I don't know what to think."

"When was the last time you saw Sophie?"

"Around ten on Thursday night when I dropped her off at her aunt's house."

"You didn't talk to her after that? No calls or texts?"

"No, sir."

"How were things when you left her? You two have a fight?"

Tom's gaze narrowed as he studied the boy's facial expressions through the glass. Dylan hesitated only infinitesimally before he answered the detective's question. "Everything was fine. We didn't have a fight."

"Let's talk about that game. Do you know the identity of the fourth player? The one who uses a cross for a symbol?"

Dylan shook his head. "We all got texts one day explaining the rules of the game and inviting us to play. I wasn't interested at first. I thought the whole thing sounded pretty stupid. But Sophie wanted to play, so I went along. I didn't see the harm. I figured she was the one who had sent those texts anyway. Seemed like something she'd dream up."

"Did you ever ask her if she was the fourth player?"

"Yeah, but she would never admit it even if she was. She likes keeping secrets."

"What kind of secrets?"

"I don't know. All kinds, I guess."

"You said you thought she might have run away. Do you know of any place or anyone she'd go to? A friend or family member, maybe?"

"No, not really. Sophie's popular at school, but she doesn't have a lot of close friends. And I know she wouldn't go to any of the Cavanaughs. She'd be afraid they'd tell her dad. Her mom's family— her real mom? They're pretty much all dead or live out of the state." He paused as if something had just occurred to him. "I don't know if this is important—"

"Everything is important at this point," Craig assured him.

The boy looked uneasy. "Her grandparents on her mom's side left her some money. She always said she was going to use the cash to leave town. Go someplace where no one could find her."

"She had access to the funds?"

"No, that's the thing. All that money from her grandparents is gone."

"What do you mean?"

"There's only a couple hundred dollars left in the account."

"What happened to the rest?"

Dylan shrugged. "Her dad told her he invested it, but Sophie didn't believe him. She thinks he used the money to pay off her stepmother's gambling debts."

Craig cast a glance toward the window. "Lauren Cavanaugh gambles?"

Dylan shifted in his chair, still fidgety. "She's hard-core, from what Sophie says. There was an incident a while back that really spooked her. Two men showed up at their house while she and her stepmother were home alone. Big, tough dudes with hand cannons. Sophie stayed inside while Lauren went out to the driveway to talk to them. Things got dicey, she said. Lauren was white as a sheet when she came back inside. Wouldn't say much about it. But a few days later, Sophie found out her money had gone missing and she put it all together. That's when she decided to go live with her aunt. There was a big bust-up over it. Sophie threatened to tell her grandfather about the missing money if her dad tried to stop her from moving out."

"Did Sophie ever see those two guys again?"

"Not that she told me."

"Can you think of anyone who may have it in

for Sophie? Someone at school, maybe? A jilted boyfriend?"

"I don't think so."

"What about one of your old girlfriends?"

Dylan had been fairly animated while talking about Sophie's problems at home, but now he shifted nervously and averted his gaze.

Craig leaned in. "Is there someone like that? Come on, kid. The best way you can help Sophie is to be honest with me."

"It's not like she'd ever do anything to hurt Sophie," Dylan mumbled as he studied the cracks in the tabletop.

"Who are we talking about? Give me a name."

Dylan glanced up, wary and defensive. "Okay, but you have to understand we only went out for a little while before Sophie and I got together."

"A name, Dylan."

"Hannah."

Craig sat back in his chair. "Hannah Tucker?"

"It wasn't serious. At least…not for me," he added reluctantly.

"What about her?"

The kid looked miserable. "I guess she was pretty upset when we broke up."

"Define *upset*."

"She wouldn't speak to me for a long time afterward. Some of my buddies said she started rumors about Sophie."

"What kind of rumors?"

"Just dumb stuff. She was mad, okay? But she got over it. We're all friends again. Like I said, she would never do anything to hurt Sophie. They're like sisters."

"Like sisters, huh?"

"Yeah."

Craig glanced down at his notes. "Anything else I should know about your relationship with Sophie?"

"What do you mean?"

"Like I said, any and everything is important at this point."

Dylan's expression grew earnest, but Tom didn't trust his sincerity. Teenagers these days were pretty sophisticated. They knew how to deceive and deflect when the pressure was on.

"Sophie is a good person," Dylan said. "People have the wrong idea about her. They think because her family has money, she's all stuck-up and stuff, but she's not. She wouldn't go out with someone like me if that were true." He placed his hands flat on the table as he leaned in. "You have to find her. I don't know if she ran away or if someone took her, but she must be in trouble. She would have called me before now if she could."

"You're sure about that?"

The kid jutted his chin. "She would have called."

"Okay, son. That's all for now. You're free to

go." When Dylan started to rise, Craig added, "Don't leave town."

Tom watched as Dylan exited the room. He'd been polite and cooperative, but something about his manner still niggled. His concern for Sophie seemed genuine, and after his initial reticence, he'd answered every question. So why was Tom's gut warning him to dig deeper? Had the kid been a little *too* obliging? A little too willing to throw Hannah Tucker under the bus?

The door opened and Craig poked his head in. "What did you think?"

"Deliberate or not, he sure painted Hannah as a person of interest."

Craig nodded. "Maybe I should call him back in and lean on him a little harder."

"Give him some time to simmer. Let's hear what Hannah has to say."

Tom returned his attention to the window as Hannah and her mother were ushered into the interrogation room. Hannah sat down at the wooden table while her mother hovered in the background. Craig introduced himself and gave Hannah a word of encouragement before he took the seat across from her.

Unlike Dylan, the girl appeared cool and collected. She sat ramrod straight in the chair with her hands folded on the table. She wore a simple sleeveless dress with a sweater tied around her shoulders. Her hair was pulled back in a pony-tail and her face scrubbed clean of makeup. She looked younger than sixteen and much more sub-dued than she had at Rae's house the day before. Restrained but not the least bit intimidated. Like Dylan, she readily admitted to her participation in the game.

"It was just a way to pass the time," she ex-plained. "Something different. We never thought anyone would get hurt or…" She trailed off on a tremulous note.

Craig projected a hint of frustration at her re-sponse. "Why didn't you mention any of this to Sheriff Brannon when you saw him at Rae Ca-vanaugh's house yesterday? Why did you lie and tell him that none of your friends went out to the Ruins anymore?"

She gazed across the table with wide, guile-less eyes. "Because we all made a pact that we wouldn't tell anyone. Sophie was afraid of what her dad would do if he found out and I didn't want to worry my mom." She glanced back at her mother. "I'm sorry, Mommy. We didn't mean any harm. It just gets so boring around here."

"We'll talk about it when we get home," her mother said. "Just answer the detective's ques-tions."

Hannah turned back to Craig. "There really

isn't much to do in this town, you know. That's why we kept playing."

"Do you know who the fourth player is?" Craig asked. "The one who uses a cross for his or her symbol?"

She shrugged. "Dylan and I both thought it was Sophie. She likes mysteries and games, and the Ruins have always fascinated her. She used to go out there after school sometimes and take pictures. I think it's because of what happened. Sophie kind of romanticized Riley's disappearance. She became a little obsessed. She used to say it was strange that she could be so invisible to her family while a girl who vanished fifteen years ago was still all any of them ever thought about."

"Did Sophie talk to you about any other problems she had at home?"

Hannah considered the question with a pensive frown. "She and her stepmother don't get along. Sophie hates Lauren. She calls her a gold-digging slut."

"Hannah," her mother reproached.

"I'm sorry, but I'm just repeating what Sophie said. She called her a lot of other things, too. If you want, I can make you a list."

"Maybe later," Craig said. "Did she ever talk about running away from home?"

"All the time. I used to think she just wanted to get her family's attention, but maybe it was something more. I don't know. Dylan wasn't much help. He egged her on."

"How do you mean?"

"Sophie inherited some money from her mom's side of the family, but she couldn't touch it until she turned eighteen. She didn't want to wait that long to leave home, so she and Dylan used to sit around dreaming up ways to get their hands on that money."

"What did they come up with?"

"Just crazy stuff. I really didn't pay much attention."

Craig's tone dropped imperceptibly. "It must have been awkward for you, listening to Sophie and Dylan make all those plans together."

Hannah's expression remained passive, but her gaze turned shrewd. "Why would you think that?"

"You and Dylan used to go out, didn't you? Wasn't there a part of you that resented Sophie? He broke up with you to be with her."

Hannah's mother moved in closer as if to warn him to tread carefully.

Hannah didn't seem to notice. Her eyes widened in surprise as she shot a glance at the two-way window. "Did he tell you that?"

"He said you were pretty upset when he called things off."

Her voice rose for the first time. "Who wouldn't

be? Do you know how embarrassing it was, the way they sneaked around behind my back? Everyone in school knew but me."

Her mother placed a hand on her shoulder. "I think that's enough for now. Hannah wants to help, but it's been a traumatic two days. I'd like to take her home *now* so she can get some rest."

Hannah swatted her mother's hand away in annoyance. "Stop it, Mommy. I'm not tired. And anyway, I've got plenty more to say about Sophie and Dylan."

Craig nodded. "I'm listening."

She sat back in her chair and folded her arms. "It's true I was angry when Dylan first broke up with me, but it wasn't long before I realized that he was much better suited to Sophie than to me."

"How so?"

She gave him a cool smile. "I plan to go to college in a couple of years and someday I'll have a fabulous career. Dylan doesn't want any of those things. He's only interested in the moment. So is Sophie, but it's totally okay for her. She doesn't have to worry about her future because she comes from money."

Was that a trace of resentment in her voice? Tom wondered.

"You told Sheriff Brannon that you talked to Sophie after Dylan dropped her off on Thursday night."

She visibly relaxed. "She texted me about our chemistry assignment and I called her back to explain something."

"How did she seem? Was she upset about anything? What was her mood like?"

Hannah paused. "She seemed distracted."

"Do you know why?"

She cast another glance toward the window, as if wondering who might be listening behind the two-way glass. "I'd rather not say. You'll think I'm just trying to get back at Dylan for what he said."

"Stick to the truth and you'll be fine," Craig assured her.

She nodded as she tightened her sweater sleeves around her shoulders. Readjusting her armor, Tom thought.

"Sophie was worried about Dylan. She said he was getting too clingy. He kept pressuring her to run away with him. Sophie's a big talker, but she's still really immature. She won't even turn sixteen until next month. Leaving town with Dylan scared her. Where would they go? How would they live without any money? She told me she wanted to break up with him, but she was afraid of how he would take it."

"Why was she afraid? Did he ever get physical with her? Threaten her?"

"No… I don't think so. But he…" She trailed away worriedly.

"What?"

"Don't get me wrong—he's a good guy," she hedged. "But he has a dark side. He used to scare me sometimes when he'd get in one of his moods."

"Did he ever threaten you?"

"No, of course not. He'd just get all mopey and quiet. I think his dad used to knock him around until he got old enough to defend himself. It's no wonder he wants to leave town so badly. I would, too, if I had a father like that."

"Are you sure Sophie didn't say anything about going out to the Ruins on Thursday night?"

"No. I knew it was her turn, but I didn't know when she would go."

"She never said anything about making a new acquaintance? You haven't seen any strangers lurking around town or school?"

She shook her head.

"And you're sure you have no idea who the fourth player is?"

"I told you, I thought it was Sophie."

Craig nodded. "Okay. Thanks for coming in." To her mother, he said, "Keep an eye on her. Make sure she doesn't leave the house without you knowing. Everyone needs to take precautions until we get to the bottom of what happened." He pulled out his card and handed it to her. "If either of you think of anything else, give me a call. In the meantime, stick around town in case we have more questions."

"Detective?" Hannah stood. "Can I ask you a question?"

"Shoot."

"Is Dylan a suspect?"

Craig gave her a direct look. "Everyone in Sophie's life is a suspect at this point. The two of you probably know her better than her own family knows her. Dylan was with her on the night she went missing and you may be the last person who spoke with her. That makes you both material witnesses. You may not think you know anything that can help us find her, but small details and seemingly irrelevant pieces of information are often how we figure out what happened. You need to think back to that last conversation. Try to remember the nuances. It's possible Sophie said something to you that could help us break this case."

She gave him a solemn nod. "I'll do my best, Detective Jarvis. Whatever it takes to find Sophie."

After she and her mother left the interrogation room, Craig lifted a quizzical brow at the window. Tom also had doubts about some of Hannah's responses. Like Dylan, she'd projected an accommodating demeanor, but it had taken her even less time to turn on him. Tom didn't trust either of those kids or their innuendos about the other.

What better way to hide a conspiracy than by casting aspersions on one's partner in crime?

# *Chapter Ten*

Shaken by that second phone call, Rae spent the rest of the morning at the ranch with her father and brother, determined to sit tight until they received further instructions from the kidnappers. That was assuming another call would be forthcoming. Doubts plagued her. What if the ransom demand was a ruse intended to keep the family from looking for Sophie until it was too late?

On and on Rae's mind spun until she became so agitated that the slightest sound caused her to jump. Her father's disposition was no better. He watched the phone on his desk with an almost unblinking focus while Jackson's mood alternated between rage and despair. Rae wasn't unsympathetic to her brother's anguish, but her patience could stretch only so far. He seemed determined to take his fury out on her, and the incessant carping wore on her nerves until she found herself sniping back at him.

He wasn't wrong. Sophie should never have

been able to sneak out of the house so easily. Rae should have kept a closer watch. But her brother wasn't without fault, either. He'd literally dropped Sophie on Rae's doorstep on his way out of town. He'd not only expected her to keep an eye on his teenage daughter, but also to take up the slack at work. Rae accepted her part of the blame, but she would allow herself to be a punching bag for only so long before she fought back.

"Rae?"

She started. Jackson had left the room for a bit and the silence had lulled her. Despite her chaotic thoughts, she'd almost drifted off to sleep. "Yes, Dad?"

"Go into town and get us something to eat."

The request surprised her. "Dad, there's a ton of food in the kitchen. If you don't want leftovers, Jetta can whip up something else."

"I gave her the day off. I couldn't stand all that hovering."

"She's just trying to help."

He scowled at Rae. "I know that. But I don't like to be fussed over. I'm not senile or at death's door like some folks like to make out."

Point taken. "Then I guess you don't want me to fix you anything, either."

He sighed heavily. "Can you just humor me for once? I want real food. Go get me the blue-plate special at the Corner Café."

Comfort food, Rae thought. Her father and his cronies often met for lunch at the café to savor Winona Landry's fried chicken, mashed potatoes and buttermilk biscuits while they argued over local politics. Under normal circumstances, Rae might have tried to steer her father toward a more heart-friendly choice, but the circumstances were far from normal and she wasn't about to intervene at a time like this. If he wanted fried chicken, so be it.

Jackson came back into the room then and Rae attempted a truce. "I'm making a run into town. Dad wants fried chicken for lunch. What about you? Can I bring you back something?"

He went straight over to the window to stare out. "I'm not hungry."

"What about for later?"

"I said I wasn't hungry, but do whatever you want. You always do anyway." He gave her a surly glance.

Rae bit her tongue. "I won't be long. I'll take the kidnappers' phone with me just in case we get another call."

Jackson returned his focus to the garden. "Let's hope you do a better job keeping up with that phone than you did with my daughter."

Rae wanted so badly to retort, but then she caught her father's eye. He shook his head slightly as if warning her to back off. She felt instantly ashamed. She was thirty-two years old, educated and accomplished by most standards, yet still in need of an admonishment from her father to do the right thing by her brother.

"Jackson?"

He turned with a scowl.

"I'm sorry I snapped at you earlier. We're all on edge. But we'll get through this. We'll pay the ransom and get Sophie back. Everything will be fine. I really believe that."

Rather than soothe, her words seemed to grate. His eyes darkened with contempt, but before he could attack, he apparently picked up on the same silent cue from their father. He flexed his hands at his sides and swallowed his anger. "I hope you're right," he finally managed.

"We can talk more when I get back if you like." Okay, that was probably overkill, Rae decided. When had she and Jackson ever had a heart-to-heart? Their fierce competition as children had devolved into a bitter rivalry as adults, one that had driven a wedge so deeply between them that Rae had no idea how to comfort her brother. The birth of his child, the death of his first wife, his promotion to CEO of Cavanaugh Industries—all milestones that Rae had let go by with little more than cursory acknowledgment because Jackson kept pushing her away.

How had things gone so wrong in their family when they'd once been so close?

Rae pondered that painful question as she pulled onto the highway. If she had to pinpoint the beginning of the rift, she would guess it to be a moment shortly before her mother's death. They all knew the end was near and had gathered around her hospital bed to say their goodbyes. Jackson couldn't take it. He'd fled the room, but they could hear his sobs from the hallway. Their father had gone after him and Rae had pretended not to overhear the ensuing conversation. Yet every now and then West's harsh words came back to her. *Stop it! You hear me? Wipe your nose and stand up straight. This is no time to lose control. You're a man now. That's not how we act.* Their mother had squeezed Rae's hand as if to say, *Take care of him, Rae. Your brother will need you when I'm gone. Riley, too. We all know you're the strong one.*

Jackson had never been the same after that day. It was almost as if he had to prove his strength to himself and to everyone around him, especially to Rae.

Tears stung her eyes at the memory and at the lost relationship with her brother. She wiped her cheeks with the back of her hand. *This is no time to lose control.*

*Just get the food and head straight home. Be*

*there for your family whether they want you
around or not.*

It was almost noon on Saturday and Belle
Pointe would be bustling with weekend shoppers.
Rae didn't relish running into anyone she knew,
but the café would be packed this time of day. No
avoiding all those sympathetic well-wishers and
pitying stares, but she would get through the ordeal as she'd always done with a bit of bravado
and sheer force of will.

Calling ahead, she was told there would be a
half-hour wait for her take-out order. She could
have easily jumped the line by giving her name
and playing the sympathy card, but instead she
left her phone number and murmured her thanks.
Killing time, she drove all around town looking
for the location where the video had been shot
even though she suspected the kidnappers were
holding Sophie somewhere remote. But she kept
searching anyway, up one street and down another.

Rae must have watched that footage of her
niece at least a dozen times trying to spot clues.
The high window behind Sophie suggested that
she could be locked in a room belowground. That
brought to mind the chilling basement at the
Ruins. The kidnappers wouldn't keep her there,
of course. The cops had been all over that place.

But what if she'd been locked away in a place equally terrifying, equally dangerous?

*Think of other abandoned places in the area. Other buildings with basements.*

Someplace close enough to the ranch that the gunshot had startled the birds from the treetops as Rae had sat shivering on the side of the road. What if she could find that place? Rescue Sophie—

*Be smart. We're watching you.*

Giving up, Rae drove back to the square and searched for a parking place. As she eased along the street, she felt curious eyes turn in her direction, but the scrutiny was mostly her imagination. Or was it? Maybe the kidnappers had followed her into town and were even now keeping a close watch on her every move.

Rae had just spotted an empty meter when she saw Dylan Moody hurrying along the street. She started to lower her window and call out to him, but he looked upset. Understandable. They were all worried sick about Sophie. However, the way he walked with such purpose—casting a glance over his shoulder before ducking into an alleyway—triggered Rae's suspicions. She told herself there was nothing unusual or nefarious about his movements. People cut through the alley all the time.

But doubts nudged her as she pulled into the

parking space and got out to feed the meter. Those
kids had been hiding something the morning
after Sophie's disappearance. Rae hadn't known
then about the game, but she'd picked up on their
sheepish behavior. They'd both lied to her face
about going out to the Ruins, so she had to wonder what other secrets they might be harboring.

Dylan seemed more approachable and far more
malleable than Hannah. Maybe if Rae asked a
few questions, she could manipulate him into giving something away. After all, she was Sophie's
aunt. It was only natural she'd want to talk to the
person with whom Sophie had last been seen. *I'll
study his face, his eyes. I'll know if he's lying.*

Right. Just the way she'd known Sophie had
been lying to her for weeks.

By this time, Dylan had vanished down the
alley. Crossing the street, Rae pretended to win-
dow-shop for a moment before heading down the
cobblestone lane behind him.

Belle Pointe was an old town, founded on the
banks of the Red River before the Civil War on
land ceded from the Caddo Indians. The area was
steeped in folklore. Rae had never bought into
any of the spooky tales. Even as a child, she'd
been too pragmatic to indulge in fantasies. But
as she crept along in the shadow of the buildings,
she suddenly remembered why the backstreet was
sometimes called Ghost Alley. As the town grew,

the prominent location of the old cemetery had become an inconvenience. Rather than moving the interred to a new resting place in the countryside, the powers that be had built over the graves. The alley between the courthouse and city hall led back to a handful of untouched graves from the original cemetery. People had sworn for years they'd seen strange lights moving up and down the alley after dark. Of course, many of them also swore they'd spotted black panthers stalking the woods and heard phantom screams echoing across the lake.

A latticework gate opened into the cemetery. The creak of the rusted hinges prickled the back of Rae's neck despite her common sense. She tried to shake off the disquiet. The local historical society tended the graves these days, but when Rae was younger, the cemetery had been a popular hangout for the three or four Goth kids in her high school. It had been more convenient than trekking out to the Ruins, and they would gather at midnight in the cemetery with candles and cheap wine. Rae had never paid them much mind. Harmless fringe dwellers, though there had been whispers of rituals and sacrifices after Riley disappeared.

Rae had never paid those rumors much mind, either. She had never been one to judge on appearances. Going by the way she looked, most would consider her a conformist, but she was a fringe dweller in her own way. Her competitive nature had always driven people away. She had no close friends and told herself she was fine on her own. Who had time for a social life anyway? But Rae suspected if she delved deeply enough, she would discover that her drive to be the best was prodded by a fear of never measuring up.

Shaking off that morose thought, she took a quick peek through the gate. No one was about. Dylan had probably used the back entrance to slip through to the other side of the alley. Rae told herself to stop this nonsense and go home. Let the police do their job. Now was the time to be with her family. What if the kidnappers called on the landline with the next set of instructions while she was out playing sleuth? She would have to drive all the way back to the ranch, and time could be of the essence.

All those things went through her mind as she entered the cemetery. It was shady inside and so quiet she could hear nothing beyond the tinkle of a wind chime and the gurgle of a small fountain. The graves, once badly neglected, were well tended now and covered in seashells. A wooden bench had been installed beneath a tree so that one could pause in the shade to rest or reflect. Rae did neither. She crossed the tiny cemetery to the rear gate and peered through the slats.

Dylan stood several yards down the alley with his back against the brick wall. His head was turned away as a silhouette approached from the street.

Rae recognized the tall, slender figure at once. The regal bearing, the catlike walk. After two years of living in Belle Pointe, Lauren Cavanaugh still stood out, even in a shadowy alley. She was like the proverbial hothouse rose in a field of daisies and dandelions. The comparison would please her, which was why Rae had always kept that observation to herself. Petty of her, but she had never pretended to be a saint.

Why was her sister-in-law rendezvousing with Sophie's boyfriend in Ghost Alley, of all places? Wasn't she supposed to be manning the phone at her and Jackson's house?

Rae wanted to believe it was simply a chance encounter, but why had Dylan paused to wait? Why did Lauren turn to glance over her shoulder? The meeting had obviously been arranged and they were taking precautions not to be noticed.

As Lauren drew even with Dylan, she placed her hand on his arm. The gesture seemed both clandestine and intimate. Rae strained to pick up their conversation. She thought at first Lauren might be comforting Dylan, but when she touched his cheek, he knocked her hand away.

Rae must have made an involuntary movement

or sound because Lauren's head snapped around and her eyes narrowed as she peered through the latticework. Quickly, Rae retreated into the cemetery, dropping down on the bench in the deepest part of the shade. A moment later, Lauren came through the gate. She didn't bother glancing around but walked straight across the cemetery to the front entrance. Maybe she'd concluded the sound had been her imagination or maybe she'd heard nothing at all. Maybe a guilty conscience had made her jumpy.

Rae wasn't sure why she didn't call out to her. Why not confront her brother's wife and demand answers? *Why are you meeting Sophie's boyfriend in an alley two days after she disappeared? Why did he lie about going out to the Ruins? Who's minding the phone in case the kidnappers call your house?*

Instead, Rae lay low, holding her breath until the gate swung closed behind her sister-in-law. Then she rose and returned to the back gate to search for Dylan. The alley was deserted. He'd already hustled out to the street, and by the time Rae returned to her vehicle, Lauren had vanished, as well.

Rae stood at the meter glancing around. Surely her sister-in-law hadn't had time to get into her car and drive off. She must have ducked into a nearby shop or restaurant. Rae could walk up and down the street searching for her through plate glass windows or she could circle the block and try to find Dylan, but what would either effort accomplish? What had she actually seen? Nothing untoward. Nothing overtly suspicious, and yet something Jackson had said to Lauren in anger came back to Rae. *Why are you defending that little creep? If I didn't know better...*

"Rae?"

Tom's deep voice jolted her out of her reverie. She glanced up. He stood in the dappled shade of an oak tree, gazing at her curiously. He wore his usual uniform of dark plaid shirt, dark tie and jeans, and her heart thudded despite her resolve. She needed to stay steady, needed to keep her distance. Needed to be mindful that someone could be watching.

When he had her attention, he approached slowly, as if worried he might frighten her away. "Sorry. I didn't mean to startle you. Whatever you were thinking about just now, you seemed a million miles away."

Rae didn't know how to respond. She felt uncomfortably lost. She couldn't bring up the kidnappers' warnings or the ransom demand. Didn't dare tell him about the burner phone or the video. But should she mention Dylan and Lauren? And tell him what, exactly? *I think they're up to something.*

He cocked his head slightly. "You okay?"

"Yes. I was just thinking about Dylan Moody. I saw him a moment ago. I wanted to talk to him, but I lost him down Ghost Alley."

"What did you want to talk to him about?" His tone sounded mildly curious, but there was a deeper emotion swirling beneath the placid surface.

*Careful, Rae.*

She shrugged, trying to arrange her features in an appropriate mask. "I just wanted to ask him some questions. That's not so strange, is it? He was the last person to see Sophie before she disappeared."

"Besides you, you mean."

"Yes, besides me. And I suppose Marty Booker saw her, too. He may also have seen Sophie's abductor, so I'm not sure why you let him go."

Tom propped an arm on the meter as he studied the street. "We don't hold witnesses in jail indefinitely unless their lives are in danger. I told you yesterday, we'll keep an eye on Marty."

"Do you know where he is now?"

"I have an officer out looking for him."

Rae said in shock, "He's disappeared?"

"His sister says he never stays in one place for too long. He'll turn up."

"I hope so."

Tom's gaze found hers. He looked cool and calm in the heat while Rae was sweating bullets beneath her shirt. It was hard to pretend not to know things with him. Hard not to blurt out the truth and plead for his help, but she'd been warned. She took herself back to that split second of terror when she thought Sophie had been shot. *Remember that. Use that. Next time could be the real thing.*

Tom took her arm unexpectedly. "I think we need to get you out of the sun. You look ready to pass out."

She jerked away. "I'm fine." His touch sent a shock wave through her battered system and she overreacted.

He dropped his hand with an apologetic gesture. "Just trying to help."

"I know." She regretted her aggressive behavior, but it was all such an impossible balancing act. *Don't get too close, but don't push him away. Don't tell him anything, but try to appear cooperative.* The strain was getting to her. Even now Tom's gray eyes seemed to probe a little too deeply and she worried about how to keep his suspicions at bay. She hadn't eaten or slept in two days. She felt too susceptible, too in need of his strong shoulder, and that knowledge distressed her even more.

For as long as Rae could remember, she'd relied on no one but herself. Even after Riley went missing, she hadn't allowed herself the luxury of a breakdown. Someone had to keep the family together. Someone had to be the rock. But what if she was no longer up to that task?

*I'm just tired*, she thought. So bone-deep weary she could hardly think straight. She wanted to sink right down to the sidewalk and bury her face in her hands. *Let someone else be in charge for a change.*

"I'm a little on edge these days," she murmured.

"If anyone has that right, it's you, Rae."

She gave him a rueful smile. "My mother would say there's never a good enough excuse for being rude. I'm sorry."

"Don't worry about it." But those stormy eyes were still watching her, still measuring her by some unknown yardstick.

Rae glanced away. "I should be getting back to the ranch. Dad will be expecting his lunch."

"Doesn't he have a housekeeper?"

"Yes, but he gave her the day off. He says her hovering makes him nervous. I drove into town to pick up some food. It should be ready by now, so if you'll excuse me..." She wiped damp palms on her jeans and told herself to stop talking.

"Before you go I need to ask about your brother."

Despite her fatigue, Rae's guard shot back up. "What about him?"

"Let's step over here out of the way." Tom took her arm to steer her into the shade, and this time she didn't object. It was hot on the street and she needed to keep a cool head.

But even as she tried to remain poised, her gaze strayed to the alleyway. What if Lauren and Dylan were somehow involved in the kidnapping? Shouldn't she say something? What if they could lead Tom and his deputies to Sophie?

A few hours ago she would never have entertained such a notion, but was it really that far-fetched? Lauren liked money. That was no secret. Her spending habits were so out of control that West had felt the need to call her out in front of her husband. *And look how she reacted to the ransom demand.* Rae had thought at the time that her sister-in-law seemed uncharacteristically emotional, not to mention desperate, in her response. *You can get the money, right? A million dollars isn't all that much by Cavanaugh standards.*

As for Dylan's part, it wouldn't be the first time a teenage boy had fallen under the spell of a conniving older woman.

Rae tried to rein in her racing thoughts. Maybe she was being a little overzealous in spinning her theory because she'd never liked Lauren in the first place.

"There you go, drifting away again," Tom said. "Where did you go this time?"

She tore her gaze from the alley. "Nowhere. What were you saying?"

He gave her a dubious look. "Are you sure you're okay?"

"I'm just worried about my dad. I need to get back home. You wanted to ask about Jackson. Can we make this quick?"

He nodded. "I want to talk to you about that argument he had with his wife yesterday. Things got pretty heated."

"Couples fight," Rae said. "They both have tempers, so petty grievances tend to escalate, even under the best of circumstances." She felt obligated to downplay the significance of the conflict even though she'd thought at the time that something more was going on between Jackson and Lauren. Everyone had secrets, it seemed— including Rae.

"Do they fight like that often?"

"I'm not with them on a regular basis, so I wouldn't know. Jackson has always been able to cut to the quick, but I doubt he gets anything over on Lauren. She keeps her claws sharp, from what I can tell." Rae paused to scan the street. They'd been standing out there for a long time. If the kidnappers were watching, they might get the wrong idea. She said impatiently, "Why do you care about that argument?"

"I care about everything going on as it relates to Sophie. You said she came to live with you because of problems at home. Lauren and Jackson certainly seem to be at odds. It must have made for a stressful home life. I'm wondering if some of their problems are financial."

He'd managed to surprise Rae again. "Why would you think that?"

"I've been asking a lot of questions for the past two days. I hear a lot of rumors."

Her voice sharpened. "About my brother?" *About me?*

"Everyone has a theory," Tom said. "There's been some talk around town about business difficulties. How are things at Cavanaugh Industries?"

Now Rae's defenses really came up. He was poking in places he had no business. Or did he? Everything was fair play when a child went missing. He would expect her full cooperation. She thought about those odd discrepancies she'd uncovered at work. Nothing truly substantial so far, but small bits of cash here and there could add up over time.

"What is it?" Tom asked.

Sunlight flickering down through the trees blinded Rae. She used the opportunity to step back, putting a little distance between them. "I'm wondering where you're going with all this."

"Just answer the question. Has there been any trouble at Cavanaugh Industries since Jackson took over?"

"A few hiccups. Nothing major. The company is fine."

"Does either of them gamble?"

Rae's brows shot up. "What? Who told you that?"

"Do they?" Tom moved out of the sun, too, closing the gap between them. His tone remained gently persistent but there was a hard gleam in his eyes that Rae had never seen before.

"I take it you don't mean the occasional scratch-off."

He shook his head slowly. "I'm talking high stakes, the kind where a bad streak can put you under for a few hundred thousand."

She gasped. "Jackson doesn't have that kind of money to lose."

"Then a debt like that could make a person desperate."

Rae stared at him for a moment. She could almost feel the color drain from her face. "You can't possibly think Jackson had anything to do with Sophie's disappearance."

"Maybe not directly. But the gambling industry attracts a dark element. The kind of lowlifes who wouldn't think twice about nabbing some-one's daughter to use as leverage."

His line of questioning and the implication of his probe worried Rae, but she took a breath and answered candidly. "I've never known Jackson to gamble. Not even on his beloved Dallas Cow-boys. That's just not his thing. As for Lauren, I can tell you that she spends money like crazy. You only have to look at the way she dresses and the car she drives to know she enjoys the finer things in life. But gambling..." Rae trailed off. "I don't know."

"You don't like her much, do you?"

"Is it that obvious?"

Tom gazed into her eyes, causing her pulse to flutter. "Put it this way. *You* should never play poker."

Was she that much of an open book? Rae swal-lowed. "Luckily, I've never been a gambler, either."

"Have you and Lauren had any trouble?"

What was behind *that* question? "We've had words on occasion. I don't like the way she treats Sophie and I think she brings out the worst in Jack-son. But mostly I try to stay out of their business."

"Except when they asked you to take Sophie in. They made her your business."

"Yes. I think we all regret that move."

His voice softened. "None of this is your fault, Rae."

"So you've said."

"She and her friends were sneaking out to the Ruins before she came to stay with you."

"Somehow that doesn't make me feel any less responsible."

"I know about guilt," he said. "I know that it can eat you up inside if you let it."

She avoided his gaze. She didn't want to see the compassion in his gray eyes. Didn't want to think about those strong arms and how good they might feel around her now. "I'll be okay. We just need to find Sophie."

"That's why I'm here. That's why I'm asking all these questions. I know they're unpleasant. I know you think my time would be better spent out beating the bushes, but anything you can tell me is important. Even something seemingly insignificant has the potential to lead us to Sophie."

Rae nodded, gulping down a sudden lump in her throat. If only he knew what she was holding back. "What else do you want to know?"

He hesitated. "Were you aware that Sophie's trust fund has been emptied?"

"I'm only vaguely aware that she has a trust fund. What do you mean it's been emptied? By whom?"

"According to Dylan, Sophie believed the money was used to pay off her stepmother's gambling debts."

So that was the reason for all the gambling questions. Rae pushed back her damp hair as she tried to square the revelation with the encounter she'd witnessed in the alley. Had Lauren tried to persuade Dylan to keep his mouth shut about the trust fund?

She gave Tom a hard stare. "I don't think I like where you're going with this. You said you didn't think Jackson was directly involved in Sophie's disappearance, but you seem to be trying awfully hard to implicate him."

"No. I'm just trying to gather as much information as possible. Like I said, we need to know everything there is to know about the people around Sophie."

"I don't know what more I can tell you."

"Let's start at the beginning with Jackson and Lauren," Tom said. "Tell me how they met."

"How can that possibly matter?"

"Maybe it does, maybe it doesn't. Think of the investigation as putting together a puzzle. You can't always know where a piece fits until you start to see the bigger picture."

She nodded with a weary sigh. "Okay. They met on vacation in the Cayman Islands. They hooked up in a bar and came back home engaged." How well Rae remembered the day Jackson had brought Lauren home to meet the family. The shock of his impetuous behavior. The uncomfortable and slightly nauseating displays of their infatuation. The mumbled congratulations that had rung hollow even to her ears. "Jackson was head over heels at first. A real goner. His first wife was lovely and sweet. The girl-next-door type. Lauren was something different, a gorgeous and exotic model, of all things. Jackson bought her a huge ring, a new house. Gave her a stack of credit cards. They seemed happy enough for a while, but things started to go south in the second year. For one thing, Sophie never warmed to Lauren. For another, Jackson led her to believe that he had money. I guess he does by Belle Pointe standards, but not ten-carat-diamond-ring money. Not three-weeks-in-an-exclusive-resort money."

"So they do have financial problems."

They were back to his original question. "I guess they do," Rae said.

He looked pensive. "Okay. That's all I wanted to know."

"Tom?" She touched his arm. It would have served her right if he'd pulled away, but instead a half smile tugged as he gazed down at her. She dropped her hand at once. "Why are you smiling?"

"I like the way you say my name."

She frowned. "What does that have to do with anything?"

"Nothing. I just like the way you say my name."

Her tone chilled. "You realize this isn't the time or place for frivolous banter."

"I do realize that. I wasn't trying to be frivolous, Rae. I meant what I said."

She shook her head, trying not to read too much into that smile, his stare. The way he said *her* name. "My niece is still missing."

"I know that."

"Is my brother a suspect?"

"Yes."

"Am I?"

"Technically."

That gave her another long pause. Then she nodded. "I understand. The family is always looked at the hardest. I remember what we went through when Riley went missing. My poor dad…all those questions he had to endure… Please don't do that to Jackson."

"I have to do my job, Rae. You know that."

"Yes, of course." She glanced out over the street. "Let me know if you need anything else. I'll help in any way I can. Right now, though, I have to get going. Dad's fried chicken is getting cold. You'll let me know if you hear anything?"

"The very minute. But you already know that."

She started back to her vehicle and then turned. He was still standing in the shade, head slightly canted, staring after her. He had the oddest look on his face, an unnerving mixture of desire, compassion and suspicion.

Why suspicion? What had she done to give herself away? Rae wondered. Was she really that easy to read or was Tom Brannon getting to know her a little too intimately?

As if intuiting her distress, he dipped his head and then turned to walk away, leaving Rae to stare after him.

# *Chapter Eleven*

Tom didn't get home that night until almost midnight. He was so tired he wanted nothing more than to fall into bed, pull the covers over his head and sleep right through his alarm the next morning. But he hadn't eaten all day, so he fixed a quick bite and then took a long shower, propping his hands against the tile wall and bowing his head so the hot water could pummel his neck and shoulders. Then he stretched out on top of the covers and stared at the ceiling while time ticked away and the quiet of the house deepened.

It had now been forty-eight hours since Rae had first called in to the station about Sophie's disappearance. The hope that she had taken off on her own volition dwindled by the minute. Still, the possibility couldn't be discounted. She had a history of running away and, according to her closest friends, had talked about it incessantly. She fit the profile. Problems at home. Craved attention from her dad and hated her stepmother.

Wouldn't be the first time a teenager had hidden out for a few days to teach her parents a lesson. But Tom didn't buy it. He couldn't imagine that Sophie would have intentionally left her cell phone behind at the Ruins. And what about those drops of blood that had yet to be identified? Too many people had motives. Too many people had secrets.

Tom had his problems with the Cavanaughs, but his heart went out to that family, especially to Rae. He knew what she was going through right now. How the guilt and worry would eat at her. The torment of her own thoughts would keep her tossing and turning all night. What was it she'd told him yesterday? *The waiting wears on you. All the terrible things that go through your head. Your mind never shuts down. You can't sleep. You can't eat.*

He pictured her pacing the floor and staring out the window. Pictured the shimmer of fear in her eyes and the soft tremor of her lips. The image made him wince. Rae Cavanaugh was the last person he should be obsessing about tonight. Nothing good could come from that distraction. Too much history and bad blood stood between them.

But he had to admit she was different from what he remembered. She could still be touchy and standoffish at times and he had no doubt she could still carry a grudge. He only had to bring up her sister-in-law's name to glimpse Rae's belligerent side. But she could also be compassionate and understanding. She'd done a lot of growing up since their high school years. Tom liked to think that he had, too. They were not unalike in a lot of respects. She worried about her family just like he did.

His sister would be thirty in another few months and Tom still felt the need to boss her around. Not that she would let him. He'd given up persuading her to move back into town. He figured she had something to prove to herself and to the monsters that chased her by living out there on the lake. He admired her courage and determination, but that didn't stop him from fretting, especially now when another girl had gone missing. What if Silas Creed really had come back? Or worse, what if a predator had roamed the streets of Belle Pointe for the past fifteen years, hiding his true nature as he mingled with his neighbors?

Tom told himself to quit borrowing trouble and get some sleep. Silas Creed was dead and gone. He wasn't coming back to Belle Pointe now or ever. Better to focus on the here and now. Every day brought new challenges to the investigation and he needed to stay sharp. But his mind wouldn't be quiet.

Rolling over, he punched his pillow as he ran

through the clues they'd uncovered thus far—
the game, the texts, the symbols. All those clandestine visits to the Ruins. The revelations about
Lauren Cavanaugh's gambling and Sophie's
drained trust fund. Hannah Tucker's sour breakup
with Dylan Moody and Rae's broken engagement
to Blaine Fenton. The rumors about Jackson Cavanaugh's financial troubles.

Tom didn't have much regard for Rae's brother,
but he couldn't bring himself to believe that anyone in the family had masterminded Sophie's kidnapping. On the other hand, Blaine Fenton had a
motive. Hannah Tucker and Dylan Moody both
had motives.

And who was the elusive fourth player?

On and on Tom's mind churned until he finally
got up, dressed and left the house. A few minutes later, he found himself pulling to the curb
in front of Rae's place. The whole house was lit
up as if she'd aimlessly flipped switches as she
wandered from room to room.

He leaned his head against the back of the seat
as he watched the windows. This was a terrible
idea. What the hell was the matter with him anyway? Even the greenest of rookies would know
better than to get personally involved with someone connected to an active investigation. Emotions only muddied the waters. He should head

back home before he was spotted, get some sleep and start with a fresh perspective in the morning.

Tom stayed put, though, because his attraction to Rae Cavanaugh wasn't the only thing driving him tonight. Maybe he was trying to justify his surveillance, but he thought she might be holding out on him, too. Keeping secrets just like everyone else. Something had changed in her demeanor and attitude from the time he'd seen her at the edge of the Fenton ranch early that morning to when he'd spoken to her in town later in the day. Something so subtle it might be nothing more than Tom's imagination, but his instincts hadn't failed him in a long time. She'd been nervous and fidgety and had a hard time meeting his gaze. He'd noticed some of that uneasiness yesterday. *What are you hiding, Rae? What aren't you telling me?*

The scent from her rose garden drifted in through his open window. The white flowers lining her walkway shimmered in the moonlight as a warm breeze whispered through the oak trees. It was one of those mild summer nights that stirred memories and aroused a dangerous longing. Tom could imagine Rae up there on her porch, toeing the swing back and forth as she watched lightning bugs flit through the dark. If he wasn't careful, he might picture himself right up there beside her.

She appeared so suddenly at one of the front

windows that Tom thought for a moment he'd somehow conjured her. But no. She was all too real as she parted the curtains and peered out into the darkness. Had she seen him? He didn't want to alarm her by his presence, so he got out his phone and sent her a quick text:

It's Tom. Just checking in to make sure everything is okay before I head home.

A few seconds went by before she answered. His text had undoubtedly caught her by surprise.

Tom? Do you have news?

No news. Sorry.

A few more beats went by before she again responded.

Are you at the station? Can't sleep. Thinking about driving over there to talk to you.

Not at the station. His thumbs hovered while he decided what else he wanted to say. I'm parked outside your house.

She reappeared at the window, cupping her hands around her face as she searched the street. A moment later, the front door opened and the porch light came on. Tom got out of his vehicle and strode up the walkway, telling himself he wouldn't linger. He'd make sure she was okay while subtly observing her behavior. Then he'd go home and get some sleep. Tomorrow would be another long day. A search party would need to be coordinated and neighborhoods would need to be canvassed. Sophie's picture would again be shown at the local bus station and it might even be time to consider bringing in some bloodhounds. But he would mention none of that to Rae unless she asked.

A neighbor's dog barked and he glanced over his shoulder, scanning the street warily before turning back to Rae. She stood silhouetted in the doorway, dressed in pajamas that would normally cover as much skin as her regular clothing, but the light from the foyer turned the cotton to gossamer. He tried not to notice the outline of her curves beneath the thin fabric, concentrating instead on her worried expression.

She folded her arms around her middle. "It's late, Tom. I'm surprised to see you tonight."

"I know and I'm sorry for coming by like this." He propped his foot on the bottom step as he gazed up at her. "I had a feeling you'd still be up."

"I lay down for a while, but I just kept staring at the ceiling and thinking about Sophie. Wondering where she is. If she's okay or if she's out there somewhere hurt and frightened. Or if she's already…gone." Her voice trailed off to a whisper. She drew a sharp breath as she glanced at the sky. "The moon is so bright tonight. I can't help but feel I should be out looking for her."

"Too risky even with a full moon," Tom said. "People tend to get trigger-happy in the dark. It's better if we wait and hit it hard in the morning."

She tucked her hair behind her ears and nodded. "It just seems like we're wasting time. It's after midnight. Sunday morning. We've entered the third day already. You know what that means."

He heard a quaver in her voice as he climbed the rest of the steps. He didn't say as much to her, but he was all too aware of that closing window. Only too cognizant of that ticking clock. "We'll find her, Rae."

"You don't know that. You said you'd do everything in your power to bring her home and I believe you. But even if you look until you've exhausted yourself and every possibility, it may not be enough. Forty-eight hours has come and gone, and you said the first twenty-four—"

"I know what I said, but Sophie isn't a little kid. From everything I've learned about her, she's smart and resourceful. A real fighter."

"Riley was a fighter, too, in her own way."

"Sophie isn't Riley."

"Everyone keeps saying that." Rae was silent for a moment. "You know the real reason I can't sleep? When I close my eyes, I see Riley reaching out to me. When I drift off, I hear her calling my name, begging me to come and find her. And then her voice fades and she's gone again. But Sophie is still out there. Maybe she's calling out to me, too. Or maybe she's already losing hope that anyone will ever come and find her."

"Rae." He didn't know what to say to her in that moment, how to comfort her without breaching ethical barriers.

She didn't give him a choice. She moved toward him and Tom just waited while she walked straight into his arms. He was so startled he hardly knew what to do. He hadn't expected this. Not in a million years. He stood stiffly as she clutched his shirt and buried her face in his shoulder. Even then, he tried to remain stoic, but he wasn't so hard-hearted or such a stickler for protocol that he could refuse her a moment of comfort. He tightened his arms around her and held her awkwardly.

"I'm sorry," she said.

"Don't be." He rested his chin on her head and held her. "It's been a rough time for all of us."

But that didn't make it okay. Not by a long shot. He was starting to feel things for Rae Cavanaugh he had no business feeling. What was he thinking, holding her like this? What was she thinking? He told himself to pull back and walk away. *Walk away.* But he couldn't bring himself to disengage. She needed a shoulder and his was right there.

A million thoughts ran through his head, none of them helpful or appropriate. She smelled really nice. Like expensive soap and shampoo. He wondered if she'd just stepped from the shower because her skin felt warm beneath her pajamas. With very little effort, he could imagine how she would look out of those pajamas, but he didn't dare let himself go there even when she slid her arms around his neck and pulled his mouth down to hers.

Tom resisted. He did. For a half second at least. But damn. She tasted like mint and hot chocolate.

He ran his tongue lightly over her lips and felt a shiver go through her. She pulled him closer, deepening the kiss with a needy little moan that set Tom's heart to pounding. He told himself, *Don't be a jerk. You have to stop this.* She was scared and vulnerable and reacting on impulse. *You can't let this happen.*

But, man, did she ever feel good pressing up against him the way she was. Lighting him up. Making him remember and forget all at the same time the last time he'd had sex.

It was that damn dog across the street that finally drew them apart. Tom lifted his head at the incessant barking and turned to search the shadows. Even then, Rae tried to pull him back in. He drew away, casting another look over his shoulder.

"This isn't a good idea."

She glanced past him to the street. "You're afraid someone will see us?"

"I've never cared too much about the gossips."

Even the ones who had speculated behind closed doors as to why Porter Brannon's children were the only ones to make it out of the Ruins that night. When Jenna Malloy had been found on the side of the road weeks later, conjecture about Tom and Ellie had eventually diminished, but by that time, the wounds ran deep. The Brannon family had learned the hard way how quickly friends and neighbors could turn, how thoroughly a small town could be divided.

"I've got a job to do," he said. "This doesn't make it any easier."

She backed away then, running a hand up and down her arm as if she were suddenly chilled. "I'm the last person who'd want to hinder the investigation."

Was she? Or was she deliberately trying to distract him?

She leaned her head against the door frame. "I

can't believe we're even having this conversation. I can't believe I kissed you."

He tried not to take her regret personally. "No harm done."

"No, I was out of line and I apologize." Her chin came up then and she met his gaze defiantly. "I don't want you to get the wrong idea. It was just a moment of weakness. My version of letting off steam."

"You don't have to apologize for being human."

She glanced away. "What happens now?"

About the investigation or the kiss?

"We keep looking," Tom said. "We keep asking questions. Someone out there saw something. They may not even know it yet. Sooner or later, that person will come forward."

Her expression was enigmatic in the shadows. "You really believe that?"

Before he could answer, the chime of an incoming text message caught her attention. He heard her gasp in the dark. Then she fumbled in her pajama pocket for her phone and glanced at the screen. A shadow passed over her features before she remembered that he was still staring down at her.

She seemed flustered. "Sorry. It's... Dad. I need to answer him..." She thumbed a quick message, taking care to position herself so that Tom couldn't glimpse the screen.

"Everything okay?" he asked.

"What? Yes. I mean, no. He can't sleep. None of us can. We're all so worried. And the memories are killing us."

Tom had his memories, too. He wanted to reassure her that everything would be okay, but missing persons cases were unpredictable, and all too often ended in tragedy. No one knew that better than Rae.

He didn't touch her again. He was careful to keep his distance. "Is there anything I can do?"

"Besides find Sophie?" She slid the phone back into her pocket and straightened, all business now that she'd had a moment to clear her head. "I didn't mean that the way it sounded. I appreciate everything you've done so far to find her. And I appreciate you coming over here to check on me. You caught me at a vulnerable time, but I'm fine now and I'd really like it if we could just forget tonight ever happened."

That might be easier said than done, Tom thought, but he nodded and said good-night. By the time he reached the bottom step, he heard the front door close. He climbed in his vehicle and circled the block, pulling to the curb a few houses down from Rae's. Another SUV was parked between his car and her house. He hoped if she looked out the window, she wouldn't be able to spy him.

A few moments later, her garage door opened and she backed her car down the driveway. Gunning the engine, she straightened the wheel and sped away. Tom waited until she made the first corner before he started his vehicle and cut his lights. He followed her all the way out to the highway, running dark and keeping a safe enough distance so that she wouldn't be able to detect him in her rearview. She took the turnoff to the ranch and he cruised on by, telling himself that she'd driven out there to be with her distressed and ailing father. Nothing suspicious about her actions. Nothing dubious about her motives. But those niggling doubts wouldn't be silenced.

He found a place to pull off the road and sat in the shadows as he contemplated his next move. He'd wait ten minutes, and if nothing happened, he'd drive back to town. He needed some rest. Tomorrow would be a day of decisions. If they couldn't pick up a trail soon, he'd have to request assistance from the Rangers and widen the search. The family would start to lose faith. Jackson Cavanaugh might even decide to take matters into his own hands and then Tom would have a real mess to clean up.

Reaching across the console, he removed a .38 from the glove box and placed it on the seat beside him. His 9 mm service weapon was locked up at home where he always kept it when he came off his watch. Maybe he was being too cautious, but it was dark and isolated where he sat. Anything could happen.

He'd started to get drowsy when the sound of a car engine brought him up sharply. He scrubbed his face as he tried to pinpoint the sound. Rae's vehicle emerged from the trees. She drove through the archway and turned left onto the highway, toward town. Tom fell in behind her, once again keeping his distance. But instead of heading to Belle Pointe, she turned right onto Lake Road.

Tom allowed more distance to creep between them. No need to keep her in sight. He knew where she was going.

RAE THOUGHT SHE'D glimpsed a vehicle behind her before making the turn onto Lake Road. Her hands gripped the wheel and she flashed another glance in her rearview. Nothing. Maybe the vehicle had been heading into town, but why would anyone be out driving this time of night without lights?

*You're seeing things*, she told herself firmly as she returned her attention to the road ahead of her. Carrying around a million dollars in cash would stoke anyone's paranoia, but she couldn't afford to get sidetracked. She couldn't afford to get careless, either. She had her instructions. She knew where and when to make the drop. The text message had laid everything out. She'd been given only thirty minutes to drive to the ranch, collect the money and then get to the Ruins.

Why there, of all places, Rae couldn't imagine. Seemed risky. Curiosity seekers might be out there even this time of night, though she thought that doubtful. She didn't relish going into the building alone—that haunted, crumbling structure where both Riley and Sophie had disappeared—but what choice did she have? Her niece's life depended on her making the drop at the appointed time and place. She'd let Riley down. She wasn't about to do the same to Sophie. But if someone had followed her from the ranch, she might have to take evasive maneuvers and that could throw off the tight timing.

Something shot across the road in front of the car. Rae had allowed herself to become too distracted by the instructions. Now she overreacted and hit the brakes while simultaneously cutting the wheel. Swerving too sharply, she lost control of the vehicle. The tires skidded off the shoulder into the ditch. The car bounced, scraped bottom and stalled.

*No! No, no, no!*

What had she done? Why, why, why hadn't she paid closer attention to the road?

Every tick of the cooling engine seemed

like the beat of a countdown clock. The night seemed to swoop down upon Rae as she sat in stunned silence. She tried the ignition, but the engine wouldn't crank. Fear and frustration overwhelmed her. She wanted to stomp the accelerator, grind the ignition and put her fist right through the windshield. How could she have been so stupid? What was she supposed to do now?

She could head out on foot to the Ruins. She'd taken the time to dress and put on sneakers, but even if she ran all the way, she'd never make it in time. The message had warned against any deviation or delay. Everything hinged on Rae getting to the Ruins in exactly—she glanced at the dash clock—thirteen minutes, and she was still at least two miles from the bridge. Then she had to climb down the embankment and follow the lake to the Ruins. The hospital had once had direct access to the highway, but that road had washed out years ago. Nowadays, there was only one way in and one way out. Aside from the history, maybe that was why the kidnappers had chosen that spot. If someone was positioned at a third-story window, he or she would be able to see Rae coming. They'd know if she was alone.

Her only choice was to call for help, but she could hardly expect her dad to come to the rescue. His heart might not be able to handle the stress, and as for Jackson...

She shuddered to think what her brother would say about her incompetence. He'd wanted to make the drop himself, but the text message had been explicit. And anyway, it was better that Rae be the one. Jackson was too close to the situation and couldn't be trusted to keep a cool head. If he came face-to-face with one of his daughter's abductors, there was no telling what he might do. Rae, on the other hand, knew when to keep her head down and follow orders. She'd make the drop and then hightail it back to the ranch to await further communication. Hopefully, in a matter of hours, Sophie would be home safe and sound and they could all put this terrifying episode behind them.

That had been the plan, but instead, Rae sat stuck in a ditch.

Despite the full moon, the thick canopy overhead blocked the light. She grew uneasy, imagining someone easing along the side of the car to ambush her. Checking the locks, she glanced in the rearview mirror. No one was there. No one had followed her. Still, she removed her dad's pistol from the backpack of money and gripped the handle. He had insisted she arm herself before leaving the house. Rae didn't own a weapon, but she knew how to shoot. Rattlers and copperheads were prevalent on the ranch. She'd never been one to go out looking for trouble, but she hadn't shied away from protecting herself and her animals.

Clutching the weapon, she scoured her surroundings. The woods seemed to close in on her. She could imagine all sorts of creatures slinking through the trees, but the only predator that worried her at the moment was the human kind.

*Just sit for a moment and let the motor cool off.*

She forced herself to count slowly to ten before retrying the ignition. Thankfully, the engine caught, and with a bit of skill and patience, she maneuvered the vehicle out of the ditch and back onto the road.

*Now take a breath and calm down.*

She could still get to the Ruins in time if she didn't make any more stupid mistakes. If she could reel in her imagination and stay focused. One step at a time. One mile at a time. She wouldn't allow herself to think about Sophie or that video. She wouldn't entertain for even a second what might have happened to her niece after the footage had been shot. For now she had to believe that Sophie was still alive. She had to get to the Ruins and make the drop. *One step at a time. One mile at a time.*

Up ahead, the trees thinned and she caught a glimpse of the bridge. Fear rippled across her nerve endings as sweat beaded between her shoulder blades. She had no idea whom or what she might encounter inside that creepy building, but she couldn't allow herself to think about that, either. Wiping clammy palms on her jeans, she told herself everything would be fine. The kidnappers were only after the money. No reason to hurt her or Sophie or anyone else so long as they got what they wanted.

Pulling to the shoulder of the road, she eased into the trees until she was certain any chance passersby couldn't spot her vehicle. Moonlight shimmered brilliantly off the lake. She wouldn't need to use a flashlight. She grabbed one anyway and tucked the pistol into the waistband of her jeans. Hitching the straps of the heavy backpack over her shoulders, she tried to keep the weight balanced as she skidded down the embankment. Twice she lost her footing and went all the way to the ground, but she made it to the bank without a broken bone or turned ankle. That was something at least.

Trudging along the treacherous path, she kept a sharp eye. Even the sound of a faint splash chilled her to the bone. She turned to search the woods. Every shadow, every movement set her heart to pounding. She wanted to use the flashlight to chase away those shadows, but she couldn't take a chance on being seen from one of the houses. So she drew another breath and plunged ahead.

The smokestack rising through the treetops

guided her toward her destination. Scrambling up the ridge, she paused momentarily to search the gaping windows. Nothing stirred. The night was very quiet, but she knew danger was only an arm's length away. She was being watched. She had no doubt that someone stood at one of those windows tracking her every move.

Adjusting the backpack, Rae headed for the same arched entry she and Tom had used on that first night. How she wished he were here with her now. How she wished she had confided in him about the ransom demand, but too late now. For all she knew, Sophie might be waiting for her inside, and that thought buoyed Rae's courage.

She waited until she was inside to turn on the flashlight, running the beam over the walls and floor and finally up to the ceiling, where Preacher stared down at her.

Moving as quietly as she could, she started up the stairs, testing each step before she applied her full weight. Then she paused at the top, once again using her flashlight to reconnoiter before she eased down the corridor. Somewhere behind her a floorboard creaked, and she whirled, her hand going to the gun hidden beneath her T-shirt. She didn't draw the weapon. Instead, she held her breath and waited. Nothing moved. Even the rats had gone silent.

She turned and continued down the corridor to

the elevator shaft. Shrugging off the backpack, she dropped it to the floor and then hovered at the edge to shine her light down into the abyss.

Glassy eyes gleamed up at her.

## Chapter Twelve

Rae teetered at the edge. If Tom hadn't grabbed her arm, he was certain she would have pitched headfirst into the shaft. She turned with a gasp, her eyes wide with terror. She tried to fight him off, and for a moment, he worried they might both lose their footing.

He clasped her wrists. "It's me, damn it. Hold still."

She froze at the sound of his voice. "Tom? What are you doing here?"

"I was wondering the same thing about you. Seems like we've been asking each other that question a lot lately."

Moonlight flooded in through the windows and the gaping roof. She looked pale and distressed as she wrested her hands from his grip. "You can't be here!"

"Why not?" He studied her in the pale light. Her fear had turned to flat-out terror. "What's going on, Rae?"

"Do you have any idea what you've done?"

"What *I've* done?" He wanted to give her a little shake, wake her up to the dangers of coming out here alone in the middle of the night where three people had gone missing. Where his own sister had been left for dead. Instead, he kept his distance and forced a neutral tone. "Seems you and I need to have a talk."

A bit of the old Rae surfaced and she looked as if she wanted to lash out at him, but then she whirled back to the shaft as a shudder ripped through. "There's a body at the bottom of the shaft."

He glanced past her to the opening. "You mean in the basement? It's not a body. We checked it out the other night, remember? It's just a pile of rags and debris."

"This is different. I saw the eyes." She swayed and he caught her elbow. "It can't be Sophie. I did everything I was supposed to."

Tom had a feeling she was talking to herself now. Pulling her gently back from the edge, he took out his flashlight and angled the powerful beam through drifting shadows until he could see all the way to the bottom of the shaft. Someone was down there all right. He spotted twisted arms and legs. A contorted face.

"Is it Sophie?" Rae asked in a fearful voice.

"No," Tom said grimly. "It's Marty Booker."

"Oh, thank God." Her hand shot to her heart. "I didn't mean... I know how that sounds. It's just..." She closed her eyes. "Thank God," she whispered.

"I know," Tom said.

She stepped back up to the rim, steadier now, but her voice was still taut with tension. "Do you think he fell?"

Tom remembered the way Marty had leaped into the shaft and agilely swung down from the rope to avoid him on that first night. The man had known what he was doing. He'd timed his jump perfectly. Why would he suddenly get careless now and miss his mark?

Putting away his flashlight, Tom reached for the rope.

"You're going down there?" Rae asked on a sharp breath. "What if *you* fall?"

"I'm not going to fall. I need to get a closer look and I need you to call 911."

His request seemed to take her aback. Her eyes widened. "But... People will come. The EMTs, cops..."

"That's the idea. We need to get that man some help. He could still be alive, for all we know." Doubtful given the twisted position of the body, but Tom had to be certain. He gave her a hard scrutiny. "What's going on, Rae? Why don't you want to make that call?"

It took some effort, but she seemed to shake herself out of that odd lethargy. Her gaze went back into the shaft as her voice softened with remorse. "I wasn't thinking. Of course I'll make the call. There's nothing else I can do right now."

He wanted to ask what she meant by that. Something was definitely going on with her tonight. Her clandestine trip made little sense to Tom, though suspicion was beginning to niggle. Outwardly, she'd quickly regained control of her nerves, but she still wasn't herself. Tom clung to the rope and wondered. Who texted her earlier when he'd stood on her front porch? What kind of message had driven her headlong out to the ranch and then to the Ruins in the middle of the night? And what the hell was in that backpack?

But those questions and all the others buzzing around in his head would have to wait until he checked the body and secured the area. "Keep your light trained downward so that I can at least see where I'm going."

He could hear her on the phone as he rappelled down the shaft. When he got low enough, he dropped to the ground with a thud and hunkered beside the body. Marty Booker's head lolled at a sickening angle. The eyes were open and staring, his hair matted with blood. Tom searched for a pulse. The skin was already cooling, but rigor mortis had yet to set in. He hadn't been dead long.

Tom gazed up into Rae's flashlight beam, shaking his head to let her know the man was gone.

Her hushed voice echoed down to him. "He's dead?"

"Looks like a broken neck."

"Then he must have fallen."

Tom wasn't so sure about that. Maybe someone had figured out that Marty Booker saw something he shouldn't have on the night Sophie Cavanaugh went missing.

Just as Tom turned back to the body, he caught a movement out of the corner of his eye. He whipped around, pinpointing a crouching shadow for one split second before the silhouette dashed for the outside steps. Tom lunged after him, dodging debris and rusty equipment before sprinting up the stairs behind him.

Arms and legs pumping frantically, the man headed in a full run toward the woods. Tom dived, hitting him square in the back, and he crashed to the ground with a pained grunt. Tom was on him in a flash, pinning his arms to his sides while he pressed his face in the dirt. All the fight seemed to go out of him then and he lay gasping for breath until Tom eased the pressure and rolled him over.

Dylan Moody threw his arms in front of him as if to ward off Tom's phantom blows. "I didn't do anything. I swear. I didn't do it." He tried to scramble away, but Tom yanked him back down.

"Just stay right where you are. Got it?"

"I didn't kill him. You have to believe me. He was dead when I found him."

Tom glared down at him in the moonlight. "Then why did you run?"

The kid looked frantic. "Because I didn't know who you were! I thought you might try to kill me, too!"

Tom grabbed his arm and hauled him to his feet. "What are you doing out here this time of night?"

"Nothing!" Dylan turned and spit blood from a cut lip, then wiped his mouth with the back of his hand. "I just came out here to look for Sophie, that's all."

Tom handed him a handkerchief. "Why did you think she'd be here?"

Dylan blotted his lip with a trembling hand. The action provoked an unexpected response in Tom. He'd been young and scared once, too, and his first inclination was to give the boy the benefit of the doubt, but there was a dead body in the basement and a girl was still missing.

"You're all right," Tom said. He doubted it was the kid's first split lip with Dwight Moody for an old man. "I need you to start talking."

Dylan spread his hands in supplication. "I was

desperate, okay? I've been out searching for her all day and I didn't know where else to look. I'd already walked the woods all the way to the river and then I went up and down the lake on both sides. I didn't find her," he added unnecessarily. "It's like she vanished into thin air."

Tom nodded toward the basement entrance. "How long were you down there?"

"Not long. Five or ten minutes, I guess. I heard voices and then I saw the body in the elevator shaft. I got scared and hid."

"You didn't see anyone else here tonight?"

"Just you."

"How'd you get here? I didn't see a vehicle out on the road."

"I left my car on the other side of the bridge. There's a place where you can pull off into the woods."

"Why take the time to hide your car if you were searching for Sophie?"

Dylan seemed stumped for a moment. "I didn't even think about that. It's where I always park when I come out here."

"To play the game, you mean."

"Yeah."

Tom's voice hardened. "That's not the real reason you came out here tonight, is it? You kids aren't still playing some kind of game."

"No. I told you. I came looking for Sophie."

Tom nodded but he was far from convinced. Something wasn't adding up. The kid seemed even more nervous than Rae. Strange how they'd both ended up at the Ruins on the same night at the same time. "You weren't afraid that whoever took Sophie might still be lurking about in those woods? Or that a property owner might see you trespassing and decide to shoot first and ask questions later?"

He met Tom's gaze straight on, squaring his shoulders as if trying to put them on equal footing. "I thought about all those things, but I didn't care. I had to look for her anyway. It's my fault she's gone."

Tom rested a hand on his belt where normally his holster would hang. Inclining his head, he stared back at Dylan through narrowed eyes. It was a stance he'd seen his dad assume many times and it had never failed to intimidate Tom. "How is Sophie's disappearance your fault?"

The kid's gaze dropped. "It's obvious, isn't it? If I hadn't agreed to play that stupid game, none of this would have happened."

"So you decided to come out here and look for Sophie in the middle of the night even though you knew the police had been over every square inch of this place for two solid days."

Dylan's gaze came back up. "The cops don't always get things right."

True enough.

Tom glanced back at the looming structure, wondering again about the timing of the night's events. At some point before Rae had entered the building, Marty Booker had fallen or been pushed into the elevator shaft while Dylan Moody had been conveniently hiding in the basement. Neither Dylan nor Rae had come clean with him yet about their real reasons for being here and he was getting a little tired of their caginess.

Just then, Rae came hurrying around the corner of the building and froze when she saw Tom and Dylan in the moonlight. Then she ran toward them.

"Dylan?" She sounded breathless and upset. "What are you doing here?" She turned to Tom. "What's going on?"

"That's what I'm trying to find out."

She came to a dead stop as if paralyzed by a sudden revelation. Then her gaze went from Tom to Dylan and back to Tom as if she couldn't quite believe what she was thinking. "Where did he come from?"

"Dylan? He was hiding in the basement."

Something flickered across her face that Tom couldn't define. "Is Marty Booker dead?"

"Yes."

She turned on Dylan. "Did you kill him?"

He shook his head violently. "I didn't kill any-one! How many times do I have to say it?"

Tom put up a hand. "Let's stay calm until we figure out what happened here."

"I think it's pretty obvious what happened," Rae said.

"What's she talking about?" Dylan asked. "Why am I being blamed for something I didn't do?"

"Keep quiet, both of you. I need a minute." Tom stepped back, making sure Rae and Dylan were in his line of sight while he called the station. In the minute or so it took him to explain the situation to the dispatcher, Rae approached Dylan and spoke to him in a low, furious tone. Whatever she said appeared to shake the kid up. He looked pale and scared in the moonlight.

"What's going on?" Tom demanded as he slipped his phone back in his pocket.

Rae's eyes were as cold as a steel moon in January. That shook Tom up. He'd never seen her look quite so much like West Cavanaugh. "I told him if you didn't make him talk, I would."

Her tone worried Tom. "I wouldn't be too hasty with the threats if I were you. He says he came out here looking for Sophie."

"And you *believe* him?"

"Is there some reason why you don't?"

She cut her gaze back to Dylan. Tom almost

expected her to lunge for the kid the way she'd gone after Marty Booker in the boiler room. Instead, she said in a deadly quiet voice, "There's only one reason he would have been down in that basement tonight. He's the one who took Sophie."

Dylan jerked back at the accusation. "*What?* No! I would never do anything to hurt Sophie!"

"I didn't say you hurt her. I said you took her."

"That's crazy! I didn't take Sophie and I didn't kill that guy in the elevator shaft. I didn't do anything but play a stupid game! You can blame me for that. I deserve it," he said in a rush. "I should never have let Sophie come out here alone. But I didn't take her. Why would I? I would never hurt her like that. I wouldn't hurt anyone."

"Take it easy." Tom could hear sirens in the distance.

Rae would have none of Dylan's denials. "You were waiting in the basement when I arrived. That can't be a coincidence."

"What are *you* doing here?" Dylan countered.

Tom turned. "That's a good question, Rae. And I'm still waiting to hear your answer."

"Ask *him.*"

"I don't know what she's talking about." Dylan stumbled back, his hands up in front of him defensively. "This is crazy. She's crazy. I'm telling you I didn't do anything."

"Just stay right where you are," Tom advised.

"If you try to run, it'll only make things worse for you."

"But I didn't do anything!" Despite the warning, Dylan looked as if he wanted to bolt for the woods. For everyone's sake, Tom decided he'd better restrain the kid. That didn't go over well. "I know what you're doing," he accused sullenly as Tom snapped on the cuffs. "You're going to pin everything on me so you can act like a big shot in town."

"Nobody's going to pin anything on you," Tom said. "This is for your own good so you don't do something stupid while we talk."

Dylan tossed his head back, trying to clear his eyes of an unruly lock of hair. "Are you going to make her tell you why she's here?"

"Stop pretending you don't know," Rae shot back.

"Okay, this is getting us nowhere fast." Tom took Rae's arm and guided her out of earshot. "He's right. I need to know why you're here. The real reason. Stop dancing around and tell me the truth."

He could see the gleam of defiance in her eyes as she lifted her chin. "Why do you keep asking me that question? He's the one you should talk to."

"I'm talking to you right now."

She snatched her arm away. "You can't possibly think I had anything to do with Marty Booker's death, let alone my own niece's abduction."

Tom kept his voice even. "I never said anything like that. But I would like to know why you decided to take a drive out here in the middle of the night. And why you don't seem to want to give me a straight answer."

As if to prove his point, she narrowed her gaze. "Why are you here, Tom? I assume you followed me, but why?"

"Are you seriously asking me that question right now?" He shook his head. "You're unbelievable, Rae. Am I going to have to take you in to get the truth out of you?"

"Take *me* in? You still have no idea what you've done, do you?"

His voice tightened. "Then tell me. I have a pretty good idea of what's going on now, but I want to hear you say it. You came here with a backpack. I saw you drop it at the edge of the shaft."

"So?"

"What's in it?"

She caved on a shudder. "Ransom money."

"Ransom money," he repeated in a level voice, but a wave of anger washed over him. That was what she'd been up to. This was what she'd been keeping from him. What the whole Cavanaugh family had been hiding from the police. Sophie had been taken for money.

Which meant the investigation had been compromised from the get-go. There was no way of knowing how differently things might have played out if Tom and his men had been given the facts. He thought of all those wasted man-hours and resources. All those futile interviews and searches. But he tamped down his frustration as he studied Rae's features in the moonlight.

"How much?"

"One million dollars in cash."

Tom lifted a brow at the amount. "You came here to make the drop?"

She nodded miserably. "Those were my instructions. I was to come alone and toss the bag into the elevator shaft from the second floor. When I got up there, I shone my light down into the basement and saw the body. I thought... Well, you know what I thought. And then I saw you and I panicked. *I was supposed to come alone, Tom.*"

"How was I to know what you were up to?"

"You could have trusted me."

"Do you really want to open that can of worms right now?"

Her gaze strayed back to Dylan. "You know what happened after that. You went down into the shaft to check the body and you found Dylan hiding in the basement. He must have been waiting for me to toss down the money. Why else would he be there? Maybe Marty saw too much and Dylan killed him."

"Let's not jump to conclusions," he said, but the kid had looked panicked as hell when Tom had tackled him.

Rae's hand crept to her throat. "I never thought of Dylan as being dangerous. He'd seemed troubled to me but was always so quiet and polite. Except his being here *can't* be a coincidence. It just can't be. What are the odds that he and I would both end up here at the same time on the same night?"

Slim, Tom had to admit.

She clutched his arm. "If he's involved in the kidnapping, then he must know where Sophie is. You have to get him to talk, Tom. You have to make him tell us where to find her."

"Oh, he'll talk," Tom said. "Don't worry about that. But I'm not through with you yet."

"What more can I possibly tell you?"

"Everything. I'm playing catch-up and we may not have a lot of time. Start at the beginning and don't leave anything out, no matter how small the detail."

"The beginning," she murmured.

"When did you get the first ransom demand?"

She didn't answer immediately, but Tom didn't get the impression she was stalling. Maybe she was just trying to get everything straight in her head. He liked to think she'd finally seen the light. Her best hope of getting Sophie back alive was to cooperate. She had to trust that he would move heaven and earth to find that girl, but he'd been working all this time with one hand tied behind his back.

"The first call came in on Friday morning on the landline at the ranch," she said. "Dad was the only one there. He said the voice was disguised but he had the feeling we were dealing with professionals. They gave him twenty-four hours to put together a million dollars. They said if any of us went to the police, they'd kill Sophie."

"Of course they'd say that."

"I know." She gazed up at him in the moonlight. "You can believe me or not, but my first instinct was to call you. Dad and Jackson refused. They reminded me that the police hadn't been able to find Riley."

"My dad couldn't find Riley, you mean."

"Please don't make this personal. We did what we thought we had to do to protect Sophie."

Tom nodded. "I get that. You had to make an impossible decision." He'd been in that position before, so he did understand. As frustrating as it was to be kept out of the loop, he couldn't honestly say he blamed Rae and her family for the secrecy. When a loved one's life was on the line, you did what you had to do to protect them. Who was he to say that he would have behaved any differently? "You said your dad was alone when he took the call. When did you find out?"

"Later that morning. He called while you were at my house. He didn't tell me anything over the phone. He just said I should get rid of you and get out to the ranch as quickly as I could. Jackson was already there and Lauren came in a few minutes later. That's when I was told about the ransom demand. Dad was naturally upset. You can imagine what we were all thinking by that time. But still he managed to call the bank and make all the arrangements. All I had to do was drive into town and pick up the money."

Tom gave a soft whistle. "He was able to arrange that much cash that quickly?"

"We've done business with Glen Stafford for years. And we have plenty of collateral." Rae shrugged. "Dad can be very persuasive when he needs to be."

"Still, it's unusual for a small branch bank like First National to have that much cash on hand. It was almost as if the money had been prearranged."

Rae frowned. "What are you getting at? You're not suggesting Glen Stafford had something to do with the kidnapping, are you?"

"I'm not suggesting anything. Just thinking out loud."

Rae wasn't buying it. She gave him a puzzled look before she continued. "I had the money in my back seat when you followed me out to the ranch. I was afraid you'd know something was wrong the moment you saw my face."

"No wonder you were so jittery," Tom said. "You almost jumped out of your skin when the phone rang."

"We thought it might be the kidnappers again."

Despite Tom's empathy, he couldn't help being disappointed in Rae's lack of faith in him. Which was ridiculous because she happened to be right. This shouldn't be personal. Still, he felt the need to press her a little. "You walked me out to my vehicle. We had a long talk about trust and yet you never said a word."

She gazed up at him earnestly, any hint of defiance or anger long gone. "Because Sophie's life was on the line! Try to put yourself in my place. She went missing from my home on my watch. I was in no position to go against Jackson's wishes. She's his only child. It was his decision to make, not mine."

"Even if it put her at greater risk?"

"There was no way we could know that. It was a gamble either way. But even then, even knowing the risk, I suggested that if we didn't trust the local authorities—you—we could go to the FBI. They wouldn't hear of that, either. So it was never about you, Tom."

"I guess that's a relief."

She bit her lip. "Look, when this is over, you can berate me all you want. We can go back to being enemies, for all I care, but right now you need to talk to that boy and find out what he knows about Sophie."

*For all I care.* "You and I aren't done," he said. Not by a long shot.

Her instinct was to argue. He could tell by the way she stood so rigidly with hands clenched at her sides, but instead of pushing back, she lifted her head as a breeze from the lake ruffled her hair. After a moment, she seemed to relax. "When I got home on Friday night, someone had been in my house. They left a phone in Sophie's room and a call came in. The person on the other end told me that if I talked to the police or the FBI Sophie would die. If I didn't come alone to the drop, I would die."

Tom's voice sharpened. "The voice specifically mentioned the FBI?"

Her gaze flickered. "Yes. Why?"

"Nothing. Go on."

"They sent a picture of Sophie bound and gagged. Her face was all scratched and bruised."

Rae faltered. "It was meant as proof of life, I guess. Or a warning."

"You still have the photo?"

"Yes, of course."

"I'll need to see it. The phone, too."

She nodded. "The photograph was hard enough to take, but the next morning after I saw you at the Fenton ranch, I was texted a video. Sophie was tied to a chair struggling to get free. The position of the window behind her made me think she might be in a basement somewhere. The footage was dark and grainy. It ended with the sound of a gunshot."

Tom tensed. "A gunshot?"

She closed her eyes on another shiver. "You can't imagine what went through my mind in that moment."

"I think I have some idea." When he'd found his sister lying facedown in the shallow water near the bank, he'd been certain she was dead. He knew about terror. He knew about panic. Any frustration he still felt at Rae's silence vanished in the face of her anguish.

"I was so terrified of what might have happened that I didn't realize at first the sound had come from somewhere in the woods instead of the video," she said. "That gunshot was a warning to me. They were near and they were watching. Maybe they thought you'd be the one I'd reach out to, so they had to do something drastic to head me off. It worked. I knew then I had to do exactly as they said. They weren't bluffing. They'd kill Sophie if I deviated from their instructions. They told me to come alone to the drop and now you're here. He's here." Her voice rose as she glanced at Dylan. "I thought I could handle myself in any situation. Keep a cool head and all that. I was so worried about what Jackson might do. He tried to come in my place, but I wouldn't let him. The kidnappers wanted me. Now I can only imagine how he'll react when he hears how badly I've messed things up."

"You didn't do anything wrong, Rae."

"Do you really think he'll see it that way?"

Tom kept his tone purposefully measured. "Let's stay calm and think this through."

"Isn't that what we've been doing?" She paused to catch her breath. "I think we can both agree our only hope now is Dylan. If he tells us where Sophie is, he can have the money. We have to get her back."

"You're still assuming he's involved," Tom said. "I'm not so sure that kid knows anything."

"He may know more than you think." She was back to being cagey again.

"Meaning?"

She lowered her voice. "I saw him in town today—yesterday—with Lauren."

Tom refused to react. "I thought you said you lost him in Ghost Alley."

"I did, kind of. But before I lost him, I saw them together. I couldn't hear their conversation. Lauren did most of the talking. She seemed very intense. When she tried to touch him, he slapped her hand away."

"Are you suggesting the two of them are somehow involved?"

"I don't know. But it wouldn't be the first time an attractive woman seduced a younger man into doing her bidding. If she's really that deeply in debt from gambling, I can only imagine how far she'd go to save her own neck. And I keep going back to the timing of all this. That Dylan would come out here looking for Sophie at the exact same time I'm making the drop is just too random. Marty Booker must have gotten in the way. Or maybe he recognized Dylan from the night Sophie went missing."

"You've got it all worked out," Tom said.

"Somebody has to." She looked instantly contrite. "I'm sorry. That just came out. Force of habit, I guess."

"Don't worry about it." But her words cut deeper than Tom wanted to admit. "Jackson seemed to think that Dylan's dad might be involved."

"Dwight?" Rae scoffed at the notion. "He's no mastermind. You think he could have come up with something as clever as that game to lure Sophie out here alone? No, it had to be someone who knew about her interest in this place. Someone who knew about Riley. They even took Sophie on the night of a blood moon. That can't be a coincidence, either."

"It's not a coincidence," Tom agreed.

"What do we do now?"

He scanned the towering facade. So many dark secrets hidden inside that crumbling building. So many ghosts still lurking in all those dark corners. If it were up to Tom, he would burn that place to the ground, but that might serve only to bury the secrets deeper. "As soon as we get some help out here, I'll send someone back inside to get the money. Not a good idea to leave a million dollars in cash lying around in an abandoned building."

"I told you, I don't care about the money. I just want to find Sophie."

"That money is your bargaining chip," Tom said.

She pounced on that. "Then you think Sophie is still alive. You think the kidnappers will call again."

He glanced back at Dylan. The kid had dropped to the ground and buried his face in his cuffed hands. "If he's involved, she's still alive. He seems to have genuine feelings for her. I don't think he'd let anyone hurt her."

"Tom." She touched his sleeve. A soft touch. An innocent touch. Yet Tom felt a brief surge of awareness in the pit of his stomach. Even after everything that had happened, he still hadn't managed to quell his desire for Rae Cavanaugh. If anything, this night had made her even more fatalistically attractive to him. How could he not admire a woman who had so willingly put her life on the line for a child who wasn't her own?

"What is it, Rae?"

"I need to call home. They'll be worried sick if they don't hear from me."

"Just wait a bit. We'll go talk to them together."

"But if they don't hear from me, they'll panic. Jackson may even drive out here to see what happened. Trust me, you don't want him anywhere near Dylan Moody right now."

Tom considered her point and nodded. "Go ahead and call, then. Tell them you're okay and you'll be home soon. But don't say anything about the ransom or Dylan or Marty Booker. Keep things brief. Understand?"

She frowned. "No, I don't understand. Why can't I tell them the truth? They'll know as soon as I walk in the door with the money."

"I'd like to be there when they find out."

A light dawned as his words penetrated. "You think someone in my family is involved."

"You're the one who told me about Dylan's tryst with Lauren," he pointed out.

"But she's not the one you're worried about, is she?"

He didn't answer, just stood there staring down at her in the moonlight. Then they both turned their heads to the sound of sirens out on Lake Road. A few minutes later, the EMTs scrambled up the embankment, followed by a small army of uniformed deputies.

He started toward them, glancing back when Rae said his name.

She looked scared and vulnerable with the Ruins looming behind her, but appearances could be deceiving. Rae Cavanaugh was not, nor ever had been, defenseless. Not for the first time, Tom paused to think about her role in all this. Did she also have suspicions about her own family? About someone closer to her than a sister-in-law? Was that why she'd stayed silent?

Like a taunt, Blaine Fenton's warning suddenly came back to him. *Don't let that pretty smile fool you, Sheriff. Way down deep, Rae Cavanaugh's every bit as cunning as her old man.*

# Chapter Thirteen

Nikki Dresden, the Nance County coroner, stood at the top of the basement steps and used the back of her gloved hand to swipe back her dark bangs. She was dressed in jeans and Converse sneakers, a far cry from the all-black outfits she'd worn with combat boots in high school. Tom had known Nikki for most of their lives, but they'd never really been friends. Even as a kid she'd been a loner. Then after both her parents split, leaving her to be raised by an aging grandmother, she seemed to have found her tribe in the small group of Goth kids who had sat at the back of the cafeteria, scribbling poetry in black notebooks as they basked in an air of perpetual gloom.

Nikki had always been smart as a whip, but somehow people were taken by surprise when she'd graduated college with honors and been accepted into the University of Texas Medical School in Galveston. However, no one had been surprised when she'd decided to specialize in forensic pathology. Death seemed right in her wheelhouse. In addition to her duties as the Nance County coroner, she also worked as a pathologist for the Northeast Texas Forensic Science Center, which served most of the rural counties in the Piney Woods area.

Tom admired the woman and all that she'd accomplished at such a young age, but he regretted the circumstances under which their paths always crossed. She hovered at the top of the basement steps, gazing up at the moon as he strode through the weeds toward her.

He greeted her with a nod. "Nikki."

"Tom."

"What's the verdict?"

"Looks like a broken neck, poor guy. He's had it rough for most of his life and now this."

"You knew him?" Tom asked in surprise.

"His family lived down the road from my grandmother for a time." She snapped off her gloves and stuffed them in her back pocket. "He also has blunt force trauma to the back of his head, but I'm not sure either injury killed him. Judging from the amount of blood on the floor and in his hair, he survived the fall. His heart was still pumping when he hit the bottom."

"What did kill him, then?"

"I noticed some faint marks on his throat. Could be thumb impression contusions. If so, the bruising will get darker in a few hours and we'll start to see evidence of asphyxiation."

"So you're saying someone crawled down into that shaft and finished him off after his neck was broken?"

"That's my gut feeling. I think you're dealing with a cold-blooded killer, Tom."

"Or a desperate one," he said. "How soon will you know?"

"I'll pull some strings and get him autopsied first thing in the morning. He deserves that. Have you notified his sister yet?"

"I'm heading over there after I leave here," Tom said. Notifying next of kin was a task he always dreaded.

"She'll take it hard," Nikki warned. "She always looked out for him when they were younger, decking any kid who dared to make fun of him. Marty never made it easy. Always getting into trouble. Always blurting out inappropriate things. Not his fault, of course. Life just plain sucks sometimes."

They both fell silent, taking a moment to remember that behind every case file was a human being.

"Tell you what," Nikki said. "I'll clear my schedule and perform the postmortem myself."

"That would be a big help. I don't want anything to slip through the cracks on this one."

"Consider it done, then."

"What about fingerprints?" Tom asked.

"You know as well as I do that it's nearly impossible to lift latent prints from a corpse. But we may be able to recover some of the assailant's skin cells for DNA testing. First things first, though. Let's get the body bagged and ready for transport. No easy feat getting him out of here."

"Have you worked out time of death?"

"Going by body temp and lack of lividity, I'd put it no more than two hours. Probably closer to an hour. You may have just missed your killer. Unless you already have him in custody." She nodded to where Dylan Moody sat on the ground with his cuffed wrists draped over his knees.

"I have my doubts about him," Tom said. "He doesn't strike me as someone who would climb down into that shaft and strangle a dying man, but I've been fooled before."

Nikki's gaze drifted to Rae. She also sat huddled on the ground, hugging her knees to her chest. As if sensing their scrutiny, she glanced in their direction, zeroing in on Tom for a moment before she turned away.

"Isn't that Rae Cavanaugh?" Nikki asked.

"Yeah, that's her."

"I see her around town now and then. She's mellowed since high school."

"Has she?"

Nikki slanted him a curious glance. "What was that look she just gave you?"

"I didn't see any look."

"Really? She seemed pretty obvious to me. I'm guessing by her presence that this has something to do with her missing niece."

"I'm still trying to put all the pieces together," Tom said. "It's a complicated case."

The coroner's voice softened unexpectedly. "It must be hard for that family going through this again. I remember when Riley disappeared. The whole town turned out to look for her."

"I remember it, too," Tom said.

Nikki lifted her gaze to scan the shadowy building. "I sat up there in one of those broken windows and watched as they dragged the lake. It felt so surreal. Afterward, the search party headed back this way and I hid upstairs until they were gone. I'm not sure why. I guess in the back of my mind I thought they might be coming for me."

"Why would they be coming for you?" Tom asked.

She shrugged. "The way I dressed, the company I kept. You don't remember how my friends and I were treated after those girls went missing?"

"I guess I had too many things on my mind back then."

"For a while the investigation took on shades

of the West Memphis Three," she said. "At least it seemed so. My friends and I even talked about leaving town. I decided to stick it out. I'm glad I did, but it was rough for a while."

"Being out here must bring back a lot of bad memories."

"You would think so, but as strange as it sounds, I've always loved this place. If you strip away all the pain and suffering, the building is really quite beautiful. Back in school, I considered it a haven. My special place. No one bothered me here. Then Riley went missing and it became her place. I guess now it's Sophie's."

"Until we find her."

"I hope that's soon."

"I hope so, too." Tom glanced at Rae. She was staring at him again. He stared right back, letting darkness spin an intimate cocoon around them.

Nikki seemed oblivious to the subtle drama. She tipped her head, gazing all the way up to the eaves. Then she seemed to shake off her dreaminess and turned back to the steps with a purpose. "I'll see you at the autopsy in a few hours. Bring doughnuts."

Tom waited until she'd disappeared through the doorway at the bottom of the stairs before he walked over to Rae. He wondered if she was feeling as anxious and off center as he was tonight. Wondered if anyone else had noticed the looks they'd exchanged and the explosion of sparks every time their gazes connected. Or was the charged air only his imagination?

She rose, clutching the backpack as he approached. "Can we go now?"

"Yes. I'll drive you home."

"I don't need a ride. I left my car on the other side of the bridge." Her tone was even, no hint of anger or censure, and yet Tom felt as if he had been subtly brushed off.

"You can pick it up later or I'll have someone drive it back to your house." He reached for the backpack. "I don't think it's a particularly good idea for you to be out driving alone with this much cash in your possession. If the kidnappers are keeping as close a watch as you seem to think, they could follow you home. Or ambush you on the way. Lots of places to lie in wait between here and the ranch."

"What makes you think they won't try it with you?"

"For one thing, they'll know I'm armed. Taking out a county sheriff is not the attention they want or need right now."

"What about Dylan?"

Tom glanced back. "We'll take him into custody and let him stew in a jail cell for a while."

"Is he under arrest?"

"Not yet, but we can hold him for a few hours

on suspicion. Maybe we'll get something out of him before he or his old man lawyers him up."

"I hope so. If we don't find Sophie soon…" She glanced away.

"I know. But nobody's giving up. Right now, the best thing you can do is go home and get some rest."

He slung the backpack over one shoulder as they started down the embankment. Rae was right on his heels. He heard her stumble once and turned to ask if she was okay. She merely shrugged and kept going.

The trek became easier once they reached the lake. She moved up beside him as they walked along the bank. The water looked silky smooth tonight, like spun silver. A light fog had begun to creep in from the other side. Tom wished he were sitting in a boat with a line cast down into those misty depths. He would have liked no more pressing business for the rest of the night than to close his eyes and remember the taste of Rae's lips as he drifted in the shallows.

Her voice brought him back with a jolt. "Do you really think someone in my family had Sophie kidnapped?"

He frowned at the water. "I told you. I'm not discounting anything at this point."

"But what a horrible thing to contemplate."

"We don't know anything yet. You have the

money and you have the phone. Let's wait and see if the kidnappers make contact again."

"What if they decide to cut their losses?" Her voice was heavy with dread.

"They want that cash. They went to a great deal of trouble to get it. They'll call."

"What should we do in the meantime?"

"We can put a trace on the landline at the ranch and use triangulation to determine the location of an incoming call on a burner. But neither action is without risk," he warned. "We don't want to scare them off."

"What would you do?"

He paused. "Let's get out to the ranch and lay all the cards on the table. The ultimate decision belongs to your brother."

A scream sounded from some distant point on the lake and Rae jumped. Her hand flew to her heart as she paused to glance over the water. "What was that?"

"A peacock," Tom said. "Something must have roused him from his roost. You've never heard that sound before?"

"Not in the dead of night." She held out her hand. "I'm shaking. I think I could do with a drink."

Tom could as well but he had a long day ahead of him. He hoisted the backpack to his other shoulder as they neared the bridge and prepared for the final ascent. They didn't speak again until they were inside his vehicle.

Rae glanced out the window with a shudder. "I hope this is the last time I ever come out here. Someone should burn that place to the ground."

"I had the same thought earlier." Tom's phone rang just then, and he fished it out of his pocket. His sister's name flashed on the screen. Why would Ellie be calling at this time of night?

He lifted the phone. "You okay?"

"I'm fine. But something's happened that I thought you should know about."

He was mindful of Rae's gaze on him. "What is it?"

"I'm outside the Thayer house. I walked over a few minutes ago when I heard the peacocks. One of them sounded in distress. I thought a fox or coyote might be after them. As soon as I came up the drive, I saw a light through one of the windows. Someone is inside the house."

"Where are you now?"

"I went back out to the road, but I can still see the house."

"Is the light still there?"

"No, it's gone out just now."

"Do you see any cars around? Anything else suspicious besides that light?"

"No. But earlier I heard a boat on the lake. There's a dock out back. Should I go check?"

"No," Tom said quickly. "You just stay put and keep out of sight. I'm two minutes away." Rae's gaze was still on him as he slid the phone back in his pocket. "That was Ellie."

"So I gathered. Is everything okay?"

"She saw a light moving around in the old Thayer house just now. I need to go check it out. Are you okay with that?"

Her gaze widened. "Do you think it could have something to do with Sophie?"

The thought had occurred to Tom as well, given the proximity of the house to the Ruins. "Let's not jump to conclusions. Probably just a squatter or someone scoping out a place to cook meth. I don't want my sister going inside alone."

"Do you think she would?"

"She might. She's quiet and introverted, but she's also headstrong."

"Then I think we should go check it out," Rae agreed. "I just hope Jackson doesn't show up at the Ruins while we're gone."

A quarter of a mile down the road, Tom killed the lights. When they were within a hundred yards of the overgrown driveway, he pulled to the side of the road and shut off the engine.

"Might be best if you wait here," he said. "Keep the windows up and the doors locked. I'll make this as fast as I can."

She gave a quick scan of their surroundings.

"I'm not staying out here alone. Weren't you the one who warned about an ambush earlier? Besides, you may need backup and I have a gun. And, yes, I do know how to use it."

Tom wasn't surprised. She'd grown up on a ranch with a father and brother who liked to hunt. And she had a point. They were miles from the Ruins, miles from help, and they had a million dollars in cash in his back seat. People committed horrible crimes for the change in someone's pocket.

He nodded. "Okay, but keep your head down."

They stayed in the shadows as they hurried down the road. When they neared the drive, Ellie slipped from her hiding place in the bushes to join them.

"I haven't seen the light since I called you," she said. "I think whoever was in there is gone. Or else lying low. No one could have gotten by me on the road. I suppose he or she could have gone through the woods or down to the lake."

"I'll check it out," Tom said. "You two stay here and keep watch. Let me know if you see anything suspicious."

"Tom, be careful," his sister warned.

Rae nodded. "Yes, be careful. And call out if you need me. I'll come running."

He saw Ellie give her a curious look in the moonlight before he turned to ease up the driveway, reconnoitering both sides of the house before he approached the porch steps. The door was locked, but one of the front windows had been broken. He slid up the frame and climbed through.

Betsy Thayer had been dead for only a few months, but already the house smelled musty and his flashlight caught the shimmer of cobwebs hanging from the ceiling. Some of the furniture remained. He traced the outlines with the beam and pinpointed the exits. Once he had the layout in his head, he started to move through the house, clearing one room at a time until he reached the back porch. He could see the lake shimmering through the bushes. If the intruder had left by boat, Ellie would have heard the motor unless paddles were used for a silent getaway.

Tom stood there on the porch listening to the night until the scream of the peacock drove him back inside. He walked through the house again, checking places he may have missed on his first pass. He came across a locked door just off the kitchen. Given the age of the house, well over a hundred years old, he imagined the narrow passage led down into a root cellar that would have also been used as refuge from the killer tornadoes that sometimes swept through the area.

He jiggled the knob and then put his ear to the door. He heard nothing and yet the hair at the back of his neck rose for some inexplicable reason. Taking a step back, he kicked the door at the weakest point and the wood frame splintered. Another kick and the door flew open. Tom fought his way through more cobwebs as he went down the steps. The basement was larger than he would have imagined for a house that size and crammed full of abandoned furniture and debris.

Against the far wall, a body lay crumpled on the floor.

Tom's heart thudded as he ran the light over the room before coming to rest once more on that motionless figure.

He said her name softly. "Sophie?"

No reaction. No movement. Dread clawed at his throat.

"Sophie Cavanaugh?"

Her head came up then and she scrambled back against the wall, mewling like a wounded kitten as she hugged her knees to her chest. "Don't hurt me. Please. I just want to go home."

Her hair was matted, her face and arms streaked with blood and dirt. Tom didn't know how badly she might be hurt or traumatized, so he approached with caution, keeping distance between them as he knelt.

"I'm not going to hurt you. I'm a police officer. My name is Tom Brannon. I'm the Nance

County sheriff. I know your folks. They're worried sick about you."

She buried her face in her arms and whimpered.

"Your aunt is outside. She's come to take you home." He slipped his phone from his pocket. "I'll call her, okay?"

No response.

Before he could use the phone, he heard footsteps above. Rae called out his name. "Tom, are you okay?"

"Down here!"

He sensed her presence at the top of the stairs and then he heard her gasp. She came down the steps so quickly he thought she might trip and break her neck like poor Marty Booker.

"You found her! Oh, my God, you found her!"

Sophie lifted her head at the sound of her aunt's voice. "Aunt Rae?"

"I'm here, Sophie. I'm here, sweet girl." She dropped to her knees and held out her arms.

# Chapter Fourteen

Sophie had been taken straight to the hospital, where she was given a comprehensive physical examination and treated for superficial cuts and contusions. Her clothing had been bagged and her fingernails scraped for trace evidence. Physically, she seemed fine and even her spirits had started to lift once her family had descended on her private room, but no one came through an ordeal like that unscathed.

Tom stood in the hallway observing the reunion through the glass panel in the door as everyone gathered around her. She sat propped against a pillow, looking wan and frail, and yet Tom had the uncomfortable notion that she was secretly basking in all that attention.

Like grim guardians, her dad stood on one side of the bed, her grandfather on the other. Rae hovered at the foot, reaching down every now and then to smooth the covers as if reassuring herself the girl was really there. Lauren Cavanaugh took her place at her husband's side, beaming down at Sophie as if she were thrilled beyond measure that her stepdaughter had been found safe and sound. But that smile didn't quite reach her eyes, Tom thought. He couldn't help remembering Rae's insinuation that something might be going on between her sister-in-law and Dylan Moody. The encounter Rae had witnessed might mean something or it might mean nothing at all. Either way, Tom intended to dig a little deeper into the woman's background.

Beside him, Craig Jarvis murmured his own reservations. "Why do I get the feeling she's secretly enjoying this?"

"You mean Sophie? I wouldn't read too much into her behavior. She's been through a lot."

Craig looked doubtful. "Were you able to get a statement?"

"We spoke briefly. She was pretty traumatized when we brought her in. I didn't want to press until she'd been examined. She says she never saw who took her. She went into the Ruins to leave her symbol on the wall and she heard a noise. When she turned toward the sound, someone grabbed her from behind and shoved a cloth to her face."

"Sounds like there were two of them," Craig said. "One distracted her while the other one nabbed her."

"Next thing she knew, she woke up in a dark,

damp room bound and gagged and with no idea how she'd gotten there. She says she was moved twice, once in the trunk of a car and once by boat. My guess is they brought her to the old Thayer house because of its proximity to the Ruins. They were keeping her close just in case anything went wrong at the drop."

"That was risky, moving her around like that."

"Probably trying to stay ahead of the search," Tom said. "It's not a lot to go on, but she may remember more once the shock wears off."

Craig gazed through the window. "Remember what Hannah Tucker said about Sophie and Dylan sitting around dreaming up ways to get their hands on her money? A ransom payoff would be a good way to get that missing trust fund back."

Tom would be lying if he said the same thought hadn't already occurred to him. "Did you get anything out of Dylan?"

"His story hasn't changed, and I leaned on him pretty hard once we got him back to the station. We'll see if he's a little more cooperative in the morning."

"Hold him for a few more hours and then cut him loose," Tom said. "But put someone on him. I want to know where he goes and whom he sees. Rae said she saw him in town yesterday with Lauren Cavanaugh."

"Lauren Cavanaugh?" Craig gave a low whistle. "That boy has more mojo than I gave him credit for."

Rae came out of the room just then and Craig conveniently disappeared. Rae took Tom's arm, drawing him away from Sophie's room. "I'm glad you're still here." The way she stared up at him caused his pulse to thump a little too erratically. "You said you would do everything in your power to find Sophie and you did. I don't know how we can ever repay you. What you've done for my family…for Sophie… There are no words."

Tom tried to play it lightly. "Ellie is the one who really found her. If she hadn't called me when she did, we might not have gotten to Sophie in time."

"I'll speak to her again," Rae said. "I want her to know how grateful we are. But you're the one who found her, Tom. You're the one."

"I did my job, Rae."

"If that's how you want to leave it, fine. But we both know you went above and beyond. I won't forget it."

"I'm just glad she's safe."

Rae's eyes gleamed suspiciously. "It's hard not to think of the past at a time like this. Hard not to remember a different outcome. But I don't want to look back. I don't want to keep wondering about what might have been. Sophie is safe. That's all that matters tonight."

Tom wanted to reach for her. To comfort her.

To tuck back her hair and kiss away her sadness. Instead, he merely nodded.

"I've carried that around with me for too long," she said. "I blamed you for what happened to Riley because I didn't want to deal with my own guilt. There were times when I wouldn't even let myself see you as a real person. It all seems so petty after everything that's happened. So trivial."

"You had your reasons, Rae."

"I thought so then. Now…" She shrugged. "I'm not under any delusions that everything will just magically blow over. Those scars run deep. But maybe with time…maybe when the dust settles… we could have coffee?"

He allowed a brief smile. "Are you asking me out on a date?"

"God, no." She wrapped her arms around her middle and shuddered. "Dating is too much pressure. Let's just call it coffee."

"Fair enough. I'll give you a call."

"Or I could call you."

"Either way." He gave in to an impulse then. Taking her face in his hands, he leaned in and planted a kiss on her forehead.

The action seemed to take her aback, although he probably hadn't startled her as much as he'd surprised himself. She pulled away, staring up into his eyes before she cupped his face and brought his mouth down to hers.

Not a good idea, Tom thought. Emotions were running a little too high, and anyway, public displays were not his thing. But with her fingers in his hair and her body swaying against his, it was a little too easy to forget they were standing in the corridor of a busy hospital.

"Rae!"

She would have jumped back at the sound of her name, but Tom held her for a moment longer, pressing his fingers into the small of her back before he let her go. West Cavanaugh stood just outside Sophie's room, his narrowed gaze pinning Tom with contempt.

"What the hell is going on out here?" he demanded.

"Nothing." Rae managed to sound perfectly normal. "Tom was just leaving."

West nodded. "Good. This is family time. Whatever questions you have will have to wait until morning."

"That's fine," Tom said. "But eventually we'll need full statements from all of you."

"Then call the house and make an appointment." West turned his attention back to Rae. "Your brother needs to see you."

"What about?"

"Sophie's decided to move back home. You don't have a problem with that, I trust."

"No. It's probably for the best, considering." She glanced at Tom. "We'll talk later?"

"Count on it."

West did not follow Rae back into Sophie's room. Instead, he remained in the corridor, glowering at Tom. "You found my granddaughter and for that I'm grateful, but it doesn't wipe the slate clean. Not by a long shot. I'll never see my youngest daughter again because of you. The hole in my heart will never be mended because of actions you took on the night of her abduction. If you have an ounce of decency left inside you, you'll leave my family alone and let us heal. Rae has a lot on her plate right now. She's likely to have more in the near future. Just step back and let her get on with her life."

Under normal circumstances, Tom would have been goaded to anger, but he kept a tight rein on his temper. "Isn't that Rae's decision to make?"

West Cavanaugh's smile turned sinister. "Don't be flattered by her attention. She's reacting to the situation. When push comes to shove, she'll do the right thing by her family. She's her father's daughter, after all. The sooner you realize that, the better off you'll both be."

AFTER TOM LEFT the hospital, he and Craig Jarvis drove over to Jefferson to inform Marty Booker's sister of his death. As the coroner had predicted, she took the news hard but agreed to meet them at the morgue to make a positive ID. After that, Tom went home to shower and even managed to catch a couple of hours of sleep before he had to be back at the morgue for the autopsy. The preliminary findings bore out Nikki's suspicions, but it would be at least a day or two before she and her colleagues reached a final conclusion. Regardless, Tom had already decided to treat Marty's death as a homicide. He'd wasted no time in getting a forensics team out to the Ruins and another to comb through the old Thayer house.

The ticking clock of a missing persons case had gone silent, but he now felt the pressure of a homicide investigation. He worked straight through two watches, leaving the station only when hunger and exhaustion finally drove him home. He ate a cold sandwich and took a hot shower, but he didn't bother lying down. He was still too keyed up. Pulling on a pair of worn jeans, he took a beer out to the front porch and sat down on the steps to enjoy the evening breeze.

The scent of roses drifting over his neighbor's fence reminded him of Rae. He wondered where she was at that moment and if she might be thinking about him.

A text message came in and then another. The deputies he had watching Dylan Moody and Lauren Cavanaugh reported in. Everything was quiet. A third ping sounded. It was Rae.

Can't sleep. You still up?

His thumbs hovered before he responded. Yeah. Can't sleep, either.

Come over.

I don't know if that's a good idea.

Come over, Tom.

He rotated his thumbs while he considered the invitation. Then he put away the phone without responding and got up to go inside.

RAE WATCHED FROM the window as Tom pulled to the curb. She waited until he got out of his vehicle and then she turned on the porch light and opened the front door. He was already halfway up the sidewalk by the time she came out to greet him. He paused with one foot on the bottom step, gazing up at her.

Emotions flitted like moths—doubts swarmed. She wondered what Tom saw when he looked at her that way. A lonely, desperate woman? He wasn't wrong. Not tonight. She'd taken care with her appearance. Styled her hair and put on a dress. Maybe she was trying too hard, and wasn't that the very definition of desperate?

He looked just right. Faded jeans, unkempt hair. Shirt only partially buttoned and untucked. So not desperate.

Slowly he climbed the steps. When he got to the top, he reached for her, drawing her into his arms, kissing her back into the house and closing the front door with his foot. Rae leaned against the wall, breathing heavily, as she toyed with his buttons.

"I didn't know if you'd come," she said.

"You knew." He smiled down at her in that way he had.

Rae slid her arms around his neck and drew him to her. "I knew."

THEY WERE IN her bedroom. Tom sat on the edge of the bed as Rae moved around the room, opening windows to the night breeze. She looked ethereal in the moonlight with gossamer curtains billowing all around her. "I smell rain."

"Storm's coming," Tom said. "Not for hours, though."

"Too bad. I like all that thunder and lightning." She lit a candle. The flame danced wildly in the breeze. Music came next and then her dress. She unzipped it slowly, letting it fall from her shoulders and puddle at her feet before she stepped out of it. She wore an old-fashioned slip, lacy and slinky, and Tom thought if he lived to be a hundred he might never again see anything so sexy.

She put out her hand and he took it, letting her draw him to his feet. She melted in his arms and they slow-danced with the shadows. He moved his hands over her back, pressing her into him, and then he tucked aside her hair to kiss her neck.

Her head fell back and she sighed dreamily. She seemed content to savor each moment, but then his hand slid up her thigh, lifting the slip, and she shivered. Drawing away, she crawled between the sheets and lay back against the pillows as she watched him undress.

He slid into bed beside her, pulling her close, kissing and stroking until she was damp and trembling. Then she took him in her hand and her mouth, and Tom thought he might have truly died and gone to heaven.

Pressing her back against the pillows, he pushed up the slip and entered her slowly as the night breeze tangled the curtains. She arched her back on a moan. He moved deeper. Deliberately rhythmic as if they were still dancing. She became frantic, digging her nails into his back as she wrapped her legs around his waist. Lifting her hands above her head, Tom paused to kiss her lips, her mouth, her breasts before he rolled them, so that she rose over him and took the lead.

On and on they moved. Kissing and straining and finally shuddering into a powerful release. Tom wrapped his arms around her quivering body and held her close.

WARM WATER SLOSHED across his naked body as Rae settled back against him in the tub. She'd lit candles again. He would never have thought of her as a romantic. She'd always seemed so pragmatic in her prickliness. But then, he would never have imagined himself as a romantic, either, and yet here he was, enjoying wine and a candlelit bath as music drifted in from the other room.

He slid down deeper in the water. "I think I could get used to this."

"Hmm. Me, too." Rae let her head loll back against his shoulder. "Better than having coffee."

"So much better."

"A week ago, would you ever have pictured us like this?"

"Not in a million years."

"It feels right, though, doesn't it? Comfortable."

Tom fidgeted as her bottom pressed into him. "I don't know about comfortable."

"Tom?"

He closed his eyes and drifted. "Yeah?"

She sat up suddenly. "Did you hear something?"

He pushed himself up and listened. "What did it sound like?"

"I don't know. The windows are still open in the bedroom. Maybe the curtains knocked over something on my dresser."

"Hopefully not a candle."

"I blew them out."

"Shush." Tom turned his head to the bedroom. Then he said against her ear, "Wait here."

He rose and stepped out of the tub, reaching for a towel as he moved toward the door.

"Tom." He glanced back where she sat shivering on the edge of the tub. She spoke softly so that only he could hear her above the music. "The pistol I had earlier is in the nightstand drawer."

"Which side?"

She motioned to his right. He nodded and turned back to the door, letting his gaze roam into all the shadowy corners before he entered the bedroom. Easing open the nightstand drawer, he removed the pistol and then pulled on his jeans. Barefoot and shirtless, he slipped across the room and out into the hallway. The music followed him all the way to the stairs. Before he started down, he glanced over his shoulder to make sure Rae hadn't followed him.

Tom wasn't a kid anymore. He had no excuse. He was a trained law enforcement officer and had been for the past ten years. Yet he never saw it coming.

The last thing he remembered before the shot rang out was the sound of Rae's scream.

# Chapter Fifteen

When Rae awakened, she found herself prone on a cold stone floor. She thought at first she'd collapsed in her bathroom. But the room she found herself in was pitch-black and the air smelled fusty, like the place had been closed up too long. She tried to sit up, but a wave of nausea crashed over her. Groaning, she fell back to the floor and drew her knees up to her chest, lying motionless with her cheek against the stone until the sickness passed and the cobwebs began to clear.

She remembered hearing a gunshot somewhere in the house and then a scream. Her own, she thought. She'd gone into the bedroom to check the nightstand. The pistol was missing. Tom must have taken it. Where was he now? She strained to remember. In her mind's eye, she saw herself picking up her dress from the floor, sliding it over her shoulders as she moved into the hallway, easing on bare feet to the banister to glance downstairs. Tom lay in the foyer in a pool of blood.

Rushing down the steps, Rae had dropped to her knees beside him. Unresponsive. No pulse. Oh, God, where was her phone? She ran back upstairs to the bedroom. Her cell wasn't on the nightstand where she always left it. She turned to scan the dresser and that was when she saw something in the mirror. A silhouette coming up behind her. She screamed and turned to fight him off, but an arm came around her, holding her close while a rag was stuffed against her mouth and nose. Her head spun. Her legs grew weak.

And now here she was in a damp, dark place…

Panic welled and for a moment Rae couldn't breathe from the fear clogging her throat. She pushed herself up, forcing back her terror as she glanced around. She could see nothing, hear nothing. She had no idea where she was.

She scrambled to her feet and shuffled forward until her extended arms made contact with a wall. Then she walked all around the room, running her hands over the stone surface until she was certain she'd explored every inch. No door. No window. No way out.

Pressing her back to the wall, she slid down to the floor and buried her face in her hands. Fear came in choking sobs. Dread tightened her lungs. Was this what Riley had experienced before she died, this paralyzing terror? *My poor little sister. My poor, sweet girl.*

Somehow the thought of Riley spurred Rae and she got to her feet, walking the room again and again searching for a way out. After a while, she started to scream. On and on until she grew hoarse and exhaustion claimed her. She dropped to the floor, throat raw and fingers bloody from scratching at the walls.

Drawing up her knees, she let herself drift into a deep lethargy. It was the only way she knew to preserve her sanity.

Tom HATED BEING so helpless. Even pushing himself up against the pillows brought a jagged pain and a wave of dizziness. He put a hand to his bandaged side and winced.

"Take it easy," Craig Jarvis advised. "You've only been out of surgery a few hours. You're lucky the bullet passed right through, but it'll still take a few days before you're back on your feet."

Tom lay back, breathing hard. He didn't feel so lucky. "Rae may not have a few days. I need to get out of here now."

"I've got every available deputy out there looking for her," Craig said. "We'll find her."

"You don't know that."

"Look, the kidnappers still want that money and we're coordinating with the family. As soon as they call, we'll arrange a swap."

"Assuming that's why she was taken."

"Why else?"

Tom turned his head to the window. "I don't know. This seems like something different."

"Different how?"

"That's what I've been lying here trying to figure out." He reached for the water beside his bed. Raising his head to take a sip exhausted him. "I need to get out of here."

"You need to rest. I'll keep you posted every step of the way. You have my word on that."

After Craig left, Tom managed to sit up, but he couldn't muster the strength to swing his legs over the side of the bed. His clothes must be around here somewhere. If he could just get to his feet—

A phone buzzed. He looked around in confusion until he spotted his cell on the bedside table. Craig must have brought it to him. Or maybe he'd had it in his pocket when they brought him in.

He reached for the phone and lifted it to his ear. "Brannon."

"I know where she is, Sheriff."

His pulse jumped. "Who is this?"

"I saw where they took her. If you want to see her alive, you'll do exactly as I say."

As IMPOSSIBLE AS it seemed, Rae had almost managed to doze off when a scraping sound awakened her. She lifted her head from her knees and glanced around her darkened surroundings. What was that? Sounded like something heavy being dragged across stone.

She lifted her gaze to the noise. To her amazement, a crack appeared in the ceiling, allowing dim light to filter down into her prison. The opening grew wider and a face appeared.

Rae jumped to her feet, pressing back against the wall. "Who are you? What do you want with me?"

"Move back," a voice ordered.

A wooden ladder dropped down, almost clipping Rae's shoulder before she stumbled out of the way.

The face appeared above her again. "Come on!"

Rae went over to the ladder and stared up into the light. "Dylan?"

"Hurry! He's coming back and I don't know how soon help will arrive."

"Who?" Rae tested the rungs and then started to climb. "Who's coming back?"

Dylan grabbed her wrists and hoisted her through the opening. "You don't know where you are, do you?"

She glanced around. They were in a barn. She could smell hay and motor oil. A welcome aroma to the dank air of her underground prison.

"That Fenton dude brought you here," Dylan said. "This is his barn."

The name shocked Rae, though she didn't know why. Hadn't Tom been suspicious of Blaine all along?

"How did you find me?"

"I've been watching him. After Sophie was taken, I started noticing things. Remembering things. Like how I saw him hanging around outside her house once. Like how he would sometimes come into the Corner Café and just stare at us while we ate."

"Why didn't you tell the police?"

"You think they'd believe someone like me? They tried to pin everything on me. I've had cops on my tail ever since I got out of jail. As soon as I managed to shake them, I came out here to look for proof."

"That was dangerous."

"I guess. But I wasn't going to let him take Sophie again. When I heard you were missing, I figured he'd have you someplace close. That's when I found the trapdoor. I think they must have built the barn over an old storm cellar. No one would ever have thought to look for you down there."

"Except you." She caught his arm. "What about Tom? Sheriff Brannon?"

Before Dylan could answer, the sound of a four-wheeler caught his attention. He swore under his breath. "He's back."

"We should make a run for it," Rae said.

"No time. We'll have to hide and hope that he doesn't check the cellar." He kicked the ladder down into the hole, shoved the cover back into place and spread a little hay over the entrance. He nodded to the loft as he got to his feet. "Up there!"

"What about you?"

"Just go!"

Rae scrambled up into the loft and flattened herself against the floor so that she could peer down through the cracks. Blaine Fenton strode into the barn a few moments later. He put aside his shotgun and then lifted his head to scan the cavernous interior as if sensing something amiss. From her vantage, Rae couldn't see Dylan. She hoped that he was well hidden. Hoped they both managed to make it out of the barn alive. To think that a man she'd once planned to marry had become a cold-blooded killer...

She wouldn't think about that now. *Keep calm. Keep quiet. Please, please let him move on.*

Instead, he moved deeper into the barn, heading straight for the cellar. As soon as he found her missing, he'd search the place from top to bottom. He'd find Dylan's hiding place and then he'd come looking for her in the loft...

A car engine sounded outside and then a door slammed. Fenton reversed course and headed back to the front of the barn, grabbing his shotgun before he opened the door to peer out.

SOMEHOW, TOM HAD managed to get up from bed, dress and make his way down to the lobby of the